The Devil in a Forest

By Gene Wolfe from Tom Doherty Associates

Novels
The Fifth Head of Cerberus
The Devil in a Forest
Peace
Free Live Free
The Urth of the New Sun
Soldier of the Mist
Soldier of Arete
There Are Doors
Castleview
Pandora by Holly Hollander

Novellas
The Death of Doctor Island
Seven American Nights

Collections
Endangered Species
Storeys from the Old Hotel
Castle of Days

The Book of the New Sun
Shadow & Claw
(comprising *The Shadow of the Torturer* and
The Claw of the Conciliator)
Sword & Citadel
(comprising *The Sword of the Lictor* and
The Citadel of the Autarch)

The Book of the Long Sun
Nightside the Long Sun
Lake of the Long Sun
Caldé of the Long Sun
Exodus from the Long Sun (forthcoming)

The Devil in a Forest

Gene Wolfe

A Tom Doherty Associates Book
New York

THE DEVIL IN A FOREST

This book is printed on acid-free paper.

An Orb Book
Published by Tom Doherty Associates, Inc.
175 Fifth Avenue
New York, N.Y. 10010

Tor Books on the World-Wide Web:
http://www.tor.com

Design by Lynn Newmark

Library of Congress Cataloging-in-Publication Data

Wolfe, Gene.
    The Devil in a forest / Gene Wolfe.
      p.   cm.
    "A Tom Doherty Associates book."
    ISBN 0-312-89032-X
    I. Title.
    PS3573.O52D48   1996
    813'.54—dc20   95-43674
                                     CIP

First Orb Edition: March 1996

Printed in the United States of America

0 9 8 7 6 5 4 3 2 1

To my children,
Roy, Madeleine, Therese, and Matthew,
and to my wife, Rosemary

"Hither, page, and stand by me,
  If thou know'st it telling;
Yonder peasant, who is he?
  Where, and what his dwelling?"

"Sire, he lives a good league hence,
  Underneath the mountain,
Close against the forest fence,
  By Saint Agnes' fountain."

—From the traditional carol
Good King Wenceslas

The Devil in a Forest

Prologue

A YELLOW-AND-WHITE dog barked savagely at the old peddler as he came up the path; but warning foxes from the farmyard was the dog's normal function, and he did not feel quite at ease barking at a man. The peddler sensed this and said, "Now, now, it's broad day," and pointed to the sun, almost perfectly poised between the dog, himself, and heaven.

The dog moved aside, still barking, to let him rap at the door.

He had already noted the new thatch of the roof and the golden generosity of the fields and had mentally sorted his pack for the finest and most costly items. The ample waist and scarlet cheeks of the woman who answered his knock confirmed his appraisal: a rich farm, a good year with the harvest nearly ready. Sweeping his soft-brimmed old wreck of a hat from his head, the peddler made a low bow beside his pack, managing at the same time to flip the throat of it open to show, obscurely, a small part of the collection of laces and ribbons he kept on top.

"Oh, madam! Would the happy chatelaine of this blessed Eden consent to spare a moment—merely—from her thousand tasks to view the finest and most reasonable stock of needles, notions, sewing and general household aids, and gown and bonnet trimmings of any ambulatory shop in the world?"

"Well"—the fat woman pursed her lips—"do you have some horn buttons? The husbandman broke one to his greatcoat, and though John the Turner's tried to match the others, his never looked quite right."

"Two hundred kinds, madam." He was already inside the door, pack and all. "Unfortunately, they are at the bottom of my bag. I have to put things there that the weight of my other stock will not break or crush, you understand, and these buttons are practically indestructible."

An hour and a half later the farmwife had a respectable pile of sundries before her, had heard all the gossip (forced wedding for the chief burgess's daughter in town, twenty yards of material at least in the skirt of the bridal dress) and news (the horse-jobber publicly whipped for selling a stolen gelding on commission for the thief) that the peddler had picked up on his travels, had told him all hers, and was watching complacently as he added up the tally marks he had scratched on one of the flagstones in the floor.

"Three broad bits eleven pence farthing," he said at length. "And I'm sure you'll agree that's not dear for all you've chosen. Furthermore"—he plunged one hand into his store of goods—"I have a special item I always reserve for an extra courtesy to good customers like yourself: a genuine stag-antler crochet hook." He handed it to her ceremoniously. "And now could I trouble you for a drink of your good well water before I go? Old as I am, carrying my pack in the heat of the day has parched me quite."

"Nonsense. I'll have the girl fetch a mug of cider and some bread and sausage." The farmwife was examining the crochet hook with obvious pleasure.

"Oh, no. No sausage. Perhaps bread and an apple or a bite of turnip with salt, if you would be so kind."

While he was munching, the peddler asked casually, "Could you tell me where that narrow road goes that turns off from the highway half a mile back?"

"Into the wilderland. There're three farms lie along it: Widow's Cruse and Shinleaf Shingle and Pyedmeadows. Then there's a village in the forest at the end of it."

"Has the village a store or a tailor's?"

The farmwife shook her head. "I haven't been there myself since I was a lass, but there's naught but a sort of monstrous inn, a cobbler's, and a blacksmith's. Gloin the Weaver lives there"—she sniffed, apparently not thinking much of Gloin—"for there're some that herd sheep where the trees don't cluster too thick, and there're charcoal burners and woodcutters. Not what you could call a real village."

"It might be a good place for me," the peddler said half to himself. "There're too many peddlers on the highroad already, and belike in such a place they'd be ready to buy."

"There's also St. Agnes' chapel," the farmwife said with an air of rectifying a prior omission, "only it's not really in the village. You go down a trifle of a path to St. Agnes' well."

The peddler retraced his route for half a mile, a thing he seldom did, and with good hope began his side trip. He made only a small sale at Widow's Cruse and found master and mistress gone at Shinleaf Shingle, but did very well at Pyedmeadows. From the top of the hill just beyond that, he could see the great mountain in the west, with the wood spreading about it, the green leaves covering the low, flanking hills and pushing back the rye fields and cattle pastures.

The sun was almost set, but he was no stranger to a bed of grass beside the road and reflected that it was better to sleep beneath the shelter of a tree than under the open sky. He would not stay at the inn unless he could beg, or at least barter, his board.

Under the shade of the first big forest chestnut he halted for a moment, straightened up, wiped his forehead on one sleeve, and shifted his pack to his other shoulder. As he took his first step forward, an arrow pierced his throat.

It was as though he had been struck a blow, and he never actually knew it was an arrow; but he saw his pack lying alongside him in the dust, and his own red blood on the road—and, for a moment, the peddler clearly saw himself as a boy running with other boys in the streets of Prague.

1

HE ABBÉ MADE the sign of the cross for the last time, sighed, and stepped backward. Old Paul the Sexton spat on his hands and began shoveling dirt into the grave, putting in a hundred times more with the first spadeful than the abbé had symbolically tossed in with his fingers a moment before.

The peddler's three mourners relaxed from their strained and unaccustomed postures of respect, put their hats back on their heads, and scratched themselves unobtrusively. Gloin the Weaver said, "Are you sure he's dead?" putting great stress on the word *sure*. He had a fear of being buried alive.

Before the abbé could reply, the sexton said, "There's no living man that would let me throw dirt in his face like that and not sit up." Since he seldom said anything at all, the three mourners perhaps accorded this dictum more weight than it merited, though it occurred to Mark, the weaver's apprentice, that when Gloin was drunk enough, neither water nor mud (which he fell into sometimes, and which is a kind of dirt, surely) seemed to have the least effect on him.

"He was dead when I found him," Cope the Smith said. "As cold as . . ." His big hands searched the air for a simile. "His blood in him was dew. Don't worry."

Cope was the biggest man in the village, and Mark thought that he might well be the biggest—if fat were disallowed—in all the world. He was as tall as the abbé (who was very tall) and far heavier, with wrists as large as Mark's thighs. His thick, curly black hair was always falling over his eyes so that pushing it back with one hand had become a habitual gesture, and though he was younger than any of them save Mark, a great bow belly thrust out past his muscular chest; a belly not soft like Josellen's father's paunch, but hard as gristle. Cope could straighten a horseshoe as effortlessly as he picked up his hammer, and Mark would have admired him tremendously if there were not a childish sullenness about him that repelled such esteem. He was the most regular worshipper at St. Agnes' chapel, and Gloin, who seldom went himself and would have attended no one's funeral without the excitement of a murder, said that whenever old Paul rang the bell Cope was in the chapel before him—though the forge was a good quarter mile from the spot where the chapel backed against St. Agnes' grotto.

Cope drank every night in Josellen's father's inn, as did all the men save the abbé, and drank more than any. But the vast draughts never made him weak and maudlin like Gloin or argumentative like Philip the Cobbler; he only became, as it were, more himself: heavier handed and slower spoken, more sullen and less attentive. It sometimes seemed to Mark, when he lay on his pallet in the webstery staring out into the village's one street, that Cope shook the ground as he went home.

Paul the Sexton was saying, "Who killed him? Why, Wat killed him, of course."

"He didn't have any money on him when you found him, did he?" the weaver asked. Both Paul and Cope ignored the question, and after a moment the abbé squinted up through the break in the trees that marked his chapel and churchyard and said portentously, "In any event, I want to see all of you—even you, Mark—in the taproom tonight. It will be a clear evening." Then, turning sharply, he strode off toward the house he shared with Paul and his wife, leaving them to wonder.

"Wat," Gloin said definitely and defiantly, "isn't the only one hereabout who has arrows and a bow."

"I wonder what Father wants," Cope said slowly.

Paul, who was still filling in the grave, ignored them both.

Clucking under his breath and shaking his head, Gloin took Mark by the arm and began to lead him back toward the village and their looms, stepping over and around the broken and leaning grave markers.

"Paul only wants to make you angry," Mark said. "You know how he is."

Gloin squinted up at the sun as the abbé had. "My boy, what time would you say it is now?"

"Midafternoon."

"Later, I should say. Nearly time to sup." Gloin hitched up his breeches. He was a spare, sickly man, lacking the monkeyish quickness of his friend Philip, who was a sparer man still. "What do you suppose the abbé wants with us all, anyway?"

"He will want me to go to my lord the archbishop with a message asking for soldiers to hang Wat. He can't go himself because there'd be no one for Sundays; Paul's too old; Cope's needed by everyone; you and Philip wouldn't do it; and one of the shepherds would just double back to his flock when he got homesick." Mark did not really believe this, but he had been thinking about it, and saying it aloud made it seem more real.

"And I wouldn't let you go," Gloin said shortly. "Anyway, the last time he went himself, and we had seven rascals quartered on us until every eatable in twenty leagues was gone, and no Wat." The little weaver spat upon the ground and appeared to become lost in thought.

The trees pressed in upon the path from the chapel to the village. Branches met above it not much higher than the abbé's head, and Mark had to walk behind his master to pass between some of the trunks. It was always shady in the forest, always humid, and almost always windless.

At the head of the path stood the great pile of the Broom and Barrel, the last building on the village street and strategically placed for pilgrims who might wish to visit St. Agnes' fountain early the next day, or who, returning from that fading fane, wished to wet their throats with something other than its icy waters. Mark saw Gloin wash his lips with his tongue tip and guessed what was coming before the weaver said it: Mark was to continue to the webstery, finish the piece now on his loom, get himself dinner, and begin carding some new wool. Gloin would sup at the inn and await the meeting the abbé had called for sunset. Mark nodded, not bothering to mention that he was also to attend the meeting, and sauntered off past the cobbler's shop until he heard the inn door slam behind

Gloin. Then he ducked behind the cobbler's and made his way through the trees to approach the inn by way of the stableyard at its rear.

The kitchen was a shed-roofed appendage of the main building. He put his ear to the door for a moment to make certain that Josellen's father was not inside smelling his dinner, and that she herself was there, before he knocked softly. She lifted the latch, looked out at him, and shut the door again. He could hear a clatter from within indicating that she had gone back to her crockery—violently, so that he would be certain to hear her. From the top of his stocking Mark drew the little Finnish knife that was his most valuable, almost his only, legacy from his dead parents, and slipped the blade between doorjamb and door to raise the latch bar. Josellen was standing with her back to him, bent over a tub of soiled plates and bowls. He knew that she knew what he had done. He called, "Josie," softly to make her turn around.

She was a short girl, and like her father not so much stocky as fleshy. The plumpness that blurred the lines of her chin and throat and distracted attention from her really fine green eyes was her worst feature; the burning red hair that spilled down her back nearly to her waist, her best. Although Mark, at fourteen, was a head taller, she looked down on him intellectually from the towering superiority of eighteen additional months.

"He'll kill you if he finds you in here, you loon."

"I'm terribly hungry, Josie. Hollow as a puffball."

"Well, nothing's near done yet." She stamped a foot theatrically. "Go hide in the stable; I'll bring you something if there's anything left."

"An apple now, Josie. I'm near starved to death."

She dipped one hand into a bin and tossed him a wrinkled survivor from the last winter's store, it no doubt having been her father's command that these be exhausted before consumption of the new crop began. He wiped away the dishwater her hand had left, scrubbing the apple on the leg of his breeches before thrusting it into a pocket.

"A bit of bread to go with it, Josie?"

She threw a wooden butter paddle at him instead, narrowly missing his head as he dodged out the door. It clattered down behind him, and a moment afterward he could hear her father calling down from the taproom to ask what the racket was.

Instead of hiding as the girl had directed, Mark cut sharply around the corner of the inn and took the short flight of steps leading to the main door two at a time, being careful to step on the front of the treads to prevent their squeaking; thus, he was able to saunter, apparently casually, into the taproom while the innkeeper was still shouting at Josellen in the kitchen.

Approaching Gloin, who was drinking a jack of ale alone at the bar, Mark knuckled his forehead. "There's naught to eat at home, master. Not a bite." Josellen's father paid no attention to him.

"Why"—Gloin pursed his lips—"there's a bit of bread in the cupboard; I'm sure I recollect leaving that from my breakfast. And some salt meat in the springhouse."

"Only the end of a stale loaf, sire." Mark was still respectful. "And the meat's rancid, master."

"Bread and salt meat and brook water." Gloin affected not to have heard him. "I'd have called that a feast when I was a lad. Here." Having seen from the corner of his eye that Josellen's father was not watching them, Gloin swiftly sliced off part of the salty cheese the inn kept on the bar for drinking customers and slipped the piece to Mark. "Now be off with you or I'll give your back a dinner that'll break the table."

Mark left quickly and proceeded along the village street until he was almost to the thatched hovel that housed Gloin and his business. He was aware that after giving him the cheese the weaver would expect him to complete his piece of worsted, and that he was not above watching from a window of the inn to see where he went. With elaborate unconcern Mark turned about and pretended to admire the view. Because the forest had been felled here to build the village, this was one of the few spots from which the peak of the Mountain could be seen clearly. The sun was setting behind it now, glinting off the ice fields at its edges and making the side facing Mark look purple. There was not too much dazzle, however, for him to see a face at one of the windows of the tap. Taking a bite of cheese, he went on.

Fortunately, the hovel had a rear as well as a front door, and Mark paused only long enough to take the bread from the cupboard. A path he himself and, to a lesser extent, Josellen had made, led along the stream behind the webstery—the village's water supply as well as its sewer— to the back of the inn. He hurried along, taking alternate bites of bread and cheese, slipped through the Broom and Barrel's stableyard gate, and secreted himself in the stable.

He barely had time to finish his apple before Josellen came in carrying an outside slice from her roast on a greasy elmwood trencher. It was of a beef that had been given only enough time to get its bearings and look about at the world before having its throat opened, and then had hung in a cool cellar; the odor of the sage and thyme in which Josellen had rolled it blended deliciously with the natural fragrance of the meat. The girl squatted beside him, watching while he cut it and forked the smoking pieces into his mouth on the point of his knife. It was nearly too hot to eat.

"Do you know what's happening?" she asked as he finished the last crisp bit of fat. "Guess who's in there now."

"Old Gloin and your father." Mark rubbed his hands on his thighs.

"The abbé and Mother Cloot just came in almost together. He hadn't hardly helloed everybody and sat himself down but what she was in at the door, and I'll tell you—I was in there bringing Cope and your master a bite of dinner—the abbé's face looked like he'd been slapped. I'll bet she followed him all the way from the chapel."

"Oh, she's harmless," Mark said. Actually, knowing that the old woman was in the village—in the very inn, in fact, in whose stable he had been eating—made him uncomfortable.

"If you want to call riding people like they were horses harmless—or flying through the air at night and sucking people's blood. She does that I'm told, and she helps girls who want to be rid of the babies in 'em; she told me herself once. And she's settin' at our bar right now with a jack before her, though"—the girl ignored her own remark of a moment before about sucking blood—"judging from the way she holds it, I don't think she's done anything but get down on all four and lap from the freshet these past twenty years."

2

ARK COULD HEAR the quick treble of Philip the Cobbler's voice before he opened the door of the taproom: "... a man that's never in all his life had a wrong thought or done a bad thing. How does your book account for that, eh? Or you take a little baby that dies ..."

The abbé, who had heard all Philip's arguments a hundred times before, said, "Ah, Mark! Now we can begin," as the boy entered. The abbé was sitting with Philip—or to be precise, the cobbler was sitting with him, and as close as possible; Philip had a tendency to argue at short range, apparently feeling that it gave him an advantage.

There was one other person at the bar, as far from the theological disputants as the room permitted; a lean and somehow wolfish-looking old woman sat on a stool near the wall. Although quite alone, she looked excited and vivacious, as if she were the center of a gay party.

The sun was well behind the Mountain now, leaving the village in a twilight that verged upon night. Josellen's father moved about the taproom lighting rushes dipped in tallow, as he did each evening. Some years since, when he and his wife, now dead, had taken the inn and changed its name to the Broom and Barrel, Philip the Cobbler had maintained that they were calling the place after themselves. Whether or not Josellen's mother had really resembled a broom Mark could not well remember, though he had a vague mental picture of a stiff, angry woman with red hair. Certainly Josellen's father, in his damp leather apron, looked like a barrel.

Gloin and Cope sat with a ragged charcoal burner at the tap's main table. Mark did not recognize the man, but his ax, the badge of his trade, lay under his stool, and his face and clothing were so begrimed as to make the identification a certainty in any case. The burners, who wandered all the forest and beyond, kept to themselves as a rule; and though their wives sometimes took carded wool from Gloin to sell back to him as spun yarn, the weaver preferred to have his spinning done by the families of the shepherds from whom he had purchased the original fleeces—saying that it made for fewer trips into the forest to buy and sell, and that the yarn came back cleaner.

This charcoal burner was a short, burly fellow with a blind eye. Apparently he had been treating, for Gloin's face was flushed and happy, and neither he nor Cope would normally sit with a burner. As the abbé cleared his throat and rapped his knuckles on the bar, Mark reflected that the burner had probably sold a load of fuel to Cope, and now felt it his duty to stand rounds.

"My friends," the abbé began, "I wish to make an appeal to your parochialism;" he smiled momentarily at his own joke. "I mean by that the love and service each of you owes your parish and its people. I had hoped to begin more auspiciously; but as most of you have heard, our host has refused my request that he clear this room." He glanced pointedly at Mother Cloot, who broke into derisive applause.

Josellen's father said in his deep, glutinous voice, "This room is open to any that have a coin to pay shot and make no disturbance."

The old woman clapped again.

"And as for you, Father," the innkeeper continued, "while you're welcome to come here, you're the last I'd let say who else might. 'Silver and gold have I none, but arise and walk,' that's you. If it weren't for Master Cope, you'd have nothing in front of you right now, and no paying customer's going to walk out on your say-so."

Mark took advantage of the argument to sidle over to the cheese on the counter. Ignoring the knife stuck in the top of it, he gouged out a portion with his fingers, keeping the bulk of the great round between himself and Josellen's father. By the time the abbé was ready to begin again, he had taken a seat at Cope's table and, with his hands concealed in his lap, was breaking off a piece small enough to smuggle up to his mouth.

"Every one of us," the abbé said, "has suffered because of Wat." He looked around the room as though inviting a challenge. "Once pilgrims flocked to St. Agnes' fountain—why do they come no longer? Why has this inn every night a score of empty beds, and why do we few sit here tonight in a great room that would hold ten times our number? Philip, weren't you once busy all day with the shoes of pilgrims while Cope performed the same function for their steeds? Gloin, don't you recall how scarves of Forest Wool—yes, and even blankets—were once carried all over the world? Now you must tramp to the town, you and Mark, to sell your work; and walk back in fear lest Wat rob you of the little you have got. For three hundred years the Vikings ravaged this land, and left a deep imprint of savagery on it. Now we think ourselves Christian men—but isn't Wat as bad as any Viking?"

The men, the charcoal burner excepted, looked at one another.

"All of us, save Mark here perhaps, remember the time the soldiers were sent after Wat. I don't believe there was a house in the village but had to sleep and feed three at least.

"Now consider! If these wanton killings continue, will not the soldiers be sent again? I do not believe, myself, that they will come because of the poor peddler we buried today; but if there is another, and another? What kind of man is it who'd shoot a poor, tired old vagrant who couldn't have resisted for a second in any case?"

He obviously did not expect an answer, but the charcoal burner rose with a sort of rustic formality. "Well," he said, "I think I know Wat better than most any here, maybe one or two excepted. We were boys together, Wat and me—not that forest boys see much of each other generally. I knew him before he took up his present occupation, and he's stopped under my roof for broth and a bite of bread"—he paused to reckon on his fingers—"three times since the snow melted this spring."

"Pardon me," the abbé interrupted, "but I don't believe I know your name?"

"And if it's all right with you, sire, I'd just as soon you didn't; we've got a statue of the Virgin we sets up wherever we burn, and that does for me and mine. She stood in Grindwalled in the old time when that was the only town there was, and this new place and the new people wasn't dreamed of.

"Anyway, lookin' about, I don't see one person excepting Mother Cloot there and my own self that's grandmother was born here in the forest."

"Me," said Cope. He held up one hand. "My mother and all her people."

"My father was a shepherd at Pyedmeadows Farm," Mark began, but the charcoal burner blew his claim to contempt with a puff of breath. "One, then, that's half forest. Well, Wat was a forest lad, and I recall well enough—my folk and his, too, has lived here since Adam left paradise— hearing 'round the fire how it was when there wasn't village here nor church, and the well was a spring folk watered sheep at."

"Then you must have heard of the miracles that took place there," the abbé said calmly. "Possibly from eyewitnesses; I envy you."

Mark had noticed a slight movement at the frame of the door opening on the kitchen stair. Now he saw a stray tendril of red hair in the doorway; Josellen was listening.

"Be that as may"—the charcoal burner surveyed the room with his one eye—"I've seen some things myself on what you might call the other side that've interested me more."

Philip the Cobbler, who had now been silent for far longer than he was accustomed to, exploded into speech. "Burn all this rubbish!" His voice was high and argumentative. "This began with a simple question: Why'd Wat kill a tramp he could've threshed out with a rotten stick? You said you could answer it; you knew Wat. So get to the point."

The charcoal burner looked abashed. "Wat's a good man," he said at last. "The most free with his friends ever I knew; not like some grab-purse shopkeepers I could put the name to. He does get spells upon him, though, when he's freer with his arrows and his knife than maybe his friends like to see him. Still, I say he's the best man and the bravest that ever walked 'round the Mountain, and there're scores in the forest who'd follow him anywhere. Sometimes a man can't stand by longer to hear himself and his folk set on by those that ought by rights to be bending their knees to them." He sat down abruptly. "Sometimes he wants to hit first."

"That's answered, then," the abbé said drily. "Wat kills defenseless old men because he is generous and brave; like St. Michael, presumably." A nervous laugh went around the room, and even Mother Cloot tittered.

"Now we just heard a good deal about Wat without learning much, but I for one should like to hear more and perhaps even learn something. How many of you have actually seen Wat yourselves? We know that he comes and goes, oppressing the roads for a time, then vanishing for months together—but how many of us have seen him? I mean besides our nameless friend?"

"I have," Philip said. "Two years past at the fair when he came in disguise. He hadn't been there an hour, so they said, when everyone was whispering his name and he had to flee; no one could have mistaken him, because the crowd all drew back and left space for him when he walked. My wife was buying a gingerbread at a stall when I heard the mob fall silent behind us—and there he was." The cobbler's eyes shone with malicious excitement.

"What did he look like?" Gloin asked his friend. Mark knew Gloin had heard the cobbler describe Wat often before, but both men enjoyed it, and Philip would be waspish if he got no chance to shine before this extensive audience.

"A tall man, powerful in all his limbs and walking erectly." The cobbler had assumed the schoolmasterish voice he usually reserved for informing the world of his unique philosophical discoveries. "His cloak muffled all his face but his eyes, pale as ice with great black brows over them. His glance"—he paused in such a way as to suggest that even he had shuddered when that glance fell on him—"was like a king's. Or like a wild beast tamer's when he strides into the cage with the clawed lions and unmuzzled bears."

"Very good," the abbé said. "Not like a king's, I should think, since a king's glance would be commanding yet serene; but very like a wild beast tamer's indeed. Like a wild beast tamer he walked coolly among a herd who had every reason to rend his flesh and had certainly the strength to do it, and he held them back with his eyes and the custom of fear and command. If you, Philip"—he looked directly at the cobbler—"had possessed the presence of mind and the courage to jostle him, or to throw a single paving stone and yell, you could have said quite honestly afterward that you yourself had slain the famous outlaw."

No one said anything for a moment; then Cope began to speak slowly and almost diffidently. "He came to me once with a mare to be shod, a black with one white stocking. I suppose she'd been stolen—she looked a good sort of animal and had been hard used before she'd lost her shoe."

He appeared to think that this was all there was to be said, but the abbé demanded brusquely, "Well, tell them about it, man."

" 'Twas last winter, Father. I had moved my bed right into the forge as I always do when it's cold, that being the warmest place. I should say it was past the midnight when he shook me by the shoulder, but 'twas not yet morning. I remember the freezing cold most of all, and going out into the road when he'd gone to look at the hoofprints in the snow by moonlight, and the way the horse steamed in the midst of my shop, cold as it was. I said, 'Wat,' soon as I saw him, before I could think that it would be better to pretend not to know him, but he only grinned like a wolf. I think he was pleased I'd guessed his name.

"He was about as tall as myself, but not so broad and thick. There was a long dagger, the work of a good swordsmith, in his belt, and a bow case and quiver on the saddlebow. His clothes were all black."

"You shod the horse?" the abbé asked.

Cope nodded. "It took a while to get the forge hot again—I had banked the fire—and he walked up and down and warmed his hands. You know how it is when a man is too used up to dare let himself sit?"

"Then he is a man for all that," Gloin exclaimed. Apparently he had previously supposed Wat to be a creature of boiled leather and brass.

"Did he pay you?" Philip put in.

Remembering his profession, Josellen's father set a fresh jack of ale before the blacksmith, remarking, "Here's a mug at the house's cost for a brave fellow. Wouldn't any of the rest of you like fresh?" Everyone did, even the abbé, laying some small coins on the bar.

"He offered to wrestle me for my money, double or none," Cope said, taking a pull at the free drink.

"Did you do it?" Philip asked. Everyone was excited.

The smith shook his massive head. "I would have beat him," he said, "and I saw it in his eyes that if I was to beat him he'd kill me. I told him no, and he gave a broad gold bit for the shoeing."

"You could have killed him," Philip said. "You could have crushed his skull with your great hammer."

Cope shook his head again; sadly, it seemed to Mark. "He would have seen the thought in me and had his knife between my ribs before I could bring myself to do it. I'm one that thinks on everything," he added slowly, "but I don't believe Wat is such as myself. He does things in the moment and laughs or cries afterward. I think he offered to wrestle all in a moment, and was glad afterward when I said I'd not."

"I believe the time has come," the abbé said when Cope had finished, "to explain why I wished to have this meeting. Cope already knows and has made certain preparations. My sexton also knows; he was to have been here but appears to have been delayed.

"I want to propose to you that we form a village *militia*; the word is from the Latin and indicates an amateur soldiery. Specifically, I propose that we who are here tonight, Mother Cloot and our friend the burner excepted, arm and organize ourselves to keep the peace in the village and on the highway and in the forest."

For several seconds the men looked at one another without speaking. Then Philip said, "I'm not saying yes or no yet. Explain what you mean."

The abbé motioned to Cope, who left the room and very shortly returned with an armload of pikes, seven-foot wooden shafts to which long iron spearheads had been affixed. Cope threw these down on the table at which he and Gloin and the charcoal burner had been sitting.

"I have reason to know," the abbé said, "that Wat usually robs alone. Sometimes he has one assistant, occasionally two; never more. Therefore we are speaking of contesting with not more than three men and more probably two or one. Counting Paul, my sexton, whom I know to be with us heart and hand, we are seven strong men. And, mark this, it is quite likely we will never have to fight Wat at all. Once he learns we are organized, armed, and determined, it is certainly possible that he will simply leave this part of the world."

A long silence followed this speech. The abbé reseated himself at the bar and took a swallow of his ale, obviously awaiting questions. Finally Gloin asked, "How can you fight someone like Wat? We can't just go out into the wood and wander around all day waiting for Wat to jump from behind a tree." Several of the others nodded.

The abbé was not in the least disconcerted by the question; he smiled at the weaver in a way that seemed to imply admiration for his foresight, and stretched out his legs. "Our exact tactics will have to be determined, of course, by the captain we will elect as our commander. I should advise, however, that our fundamental method be as follows: Let us have some regularly appointed time and place for meetings at which we will practice pike drill and plan our future operations. Let us also hang up a gong or triangle—something loud enough to be heard by Paul and myself at the chapel—somewhere near the center of the village. Then when any of us, or any woman or child, discovers a crime or other evidence that Wat has been in the vicinity, the alarm can be sounded and we can all assemble quickly with our weapons and set off on the track. For emphasis let me repeat that the exact details will have to be decided upon by the captain."

"I thought you were going to be captain yourself," Gloin said. He sounded unsettled, and it was plain that he had followed the abbé's speech no farther than the first mention of an elected commander.

The abbé shook his head gravely. "As a man of the cloth, I could not possibly accept a post at the head of a semimilitary organization such as we propose to form."

Philip the Cobbler cackled rudely.

"I should be delighted, however, to accept the position of chaplain; although my religious profession bars me from shedding blood, I would undertake to accompany all your expeditions and to carry a pike wherewith to defend myself in the event of fighting."

This seemed so fairly said, and it was so apparent that the abbé intended to stretch his scruples to the utmost, that even the cobbler looked abashed.

"I shouldn't suppose it's any of my cuttin'," the charcoal burner interjected at length, "but if you're not going to play at bellwether, who is?"

The abbé stood again. "As I said, the captain should be elected. Since it is I who will be yielding the chair, so to speak, may I have the group's leave to make the first nomination?"

Everyone nodded and looked at Cope.

"Then I nominate"—the abbé drew a deep breath—
"Master Philip, the cobbler of our village. He is a married
man of substance. He has a ready wit, a bottom of sound
good sense, and I believe as strong a heart as any of us. Are
there any other nominations?"

Cope said in a relieved voice, "Let's end the nominations." Philip looked too surprised to say anything.

"Then if no one objects, they are closed. But let us poll
the group to make certain everyone is agreeable. Master
Gloin, are you agreed?"

The weaver said, "Philip's fine with me."

"Master Cope?"

The blacksmith nodded.

"Young Mark?"

Mark nodded too. After an instant of bewilderment he
was beginning to see the wisdom of the abbé's arrange-
ment. Ordinarily Philip would have been certain to carp
at every detail, and object to every order given by whoever
led the group. As leader himself, he would have to chan-
nel his discontent toward Wat, and he was already beginning to swell and to square his thin shoulders in soldierly
fashion.

"And our good host?"

Josellen's father had resumed his place behind the bar,
from which he had followed the proceedings with the calm
detachment peculiar to his profession. Now he seemed
startled at being addressed directly. Taking his hands from
under his apron, he laid both palms flat on the wood, as
though to steady himself in the unaccustomed whirl of a
social contact with his patrons that was not ritualized and
traditional.

"No," he said.

The abbé smiled. "If you wish to nominate another candidate, that is certainly your right."

"I mean," the innkeeper said slowly, "that I'm no part of this foolishness. Now don't take that wrong." He held out his hands, large, white, and soft, in supplication; an honest and reasonable man seeking to be heard reasonably. "This is a fine thing you're doing. I wish you luck, and if you'd like to hold your meetings right here in my tap, you'll be very welcome. But as to hunting bandits in the wood and leaving my inn to anyone that comes questing down the road or out of the trees, I won't do it."

For the first time that evening the abbé seemed taken aback. Philip went white, looking from the abbé to Cope, whose broad face was slowly growing dark with anger, as though in search of support for an attack on the innkeeper's person.

It was his master who astonished Mark. Gloin rose a little unsteadily and walked—paced might be a better description, for he moved like a player portraying one of the less pleasant Roman emperors—to that part of the bar holding the "public" cheese. Disdaining any knife, he took up the entire salty, blue-mottled mass and broke it into two nearly equal halves, allowing a shower of crumbs to drop to the floor. With the smaller of the halves he marched back to the table, broke it again, and handed one of the resulting quarter cheeses to Mark.

"I suppose," said Philip the Cobbler, addressing the abbé, his voice ceremonious, "that seeing I've received the votes of all the members that are here, and that's all but Paul, I'm now the captain of the militia?"

The abbé nodded.

"Then I have a few things to say. You let this one-eyed burner here hear everything we were doing, and at first I thought that was a muttonheaded thing to do, seeing as how he says himself he's a friend of Wat's. Later on I saw you wanted Wat to know, and I think you were right about that; it's better that way—then both sides know what's happening. Now I've got something to say to him particular: Burner, you tell Wat that he can rob this inn here, or burn it down, or do anything to it he likes, without having to worry about my militia. We ain't going to raise a hand to stop him.

"Now," he addressed the meeting at large, "I mean to have a firelight pike drill to celebrate the founding of the militia and settle for certain where we're going to hang the alarm bell. Everybody take a brand out of the fire and carry it outside, and you, Mark, you bring out an armload of wood."

Josellen's father started to protest as Mark, very favorably disposed to all the excitement, gathered up a double armful of his firewood; then father saw it was hopeless and desisted. Outside, the apprentice piled the fagots in the road in front of Philip's shop, and the men thrust their brands among them to produce a leaping blaze that was soon much larger than the little fire in the taproom. With the coming of autumn the nights were growing chill in the forest, and everyone gathered around the fire for a moment to warm themselves as the flames sprang up.

Suddenly the abbé was shouting—and pointing, it seemed to the others, at the roof of the inn.

"What is it?" Philip demanded, full of new-fledged authority.

"That red light! See it? Where there are no other stars."

Mark saw it too then, a tiny crimson glimmer visible just above the peak of the inn's rooftree, alone in a black part of the sky where no other light shone. After a moment he realized why no other stars were visible there.

"Someone has built a fire," the abbé said, "at the top of the Mountain." Before any of the others could ask what he was about, the priest was running back toward the inn, holding up his habit with both hands as he went up the steps like a woman running in skirts. After two breaths he reappeared in the doorway. "Mother Cloot's gone," he called.

3

LOIN HAD A bedroom for himself in the back of the shop, but Mark slept on a pallet on the worktable in the webstery. Lying on the table instead of the floor at least kept him out of the drafts, and it allowed him to look out of the front window (something he was extremely fond of) when it was not too cold to sleep with the shutters open. Tonight the shutters were closed, and he had covered himself with most of the finished cloth in the shop and lay snug under the heap of soft woolens with only his nose and eyes and a tangle of pale hair showing.

Outside the road was silent and dark. Tomorrow he would use his knife to cut his sign on the shaft of his militia pike. The abbé had scratched the letters for him once in the dirt of the chapel path; he had forgotten just how it looked—though he remembered the two mountains at the front—but he felt certain the abbé would show him again if he asked.

Gloin would give him a shawl tomorrow and tell him

to sell it somewhere for a breakfast and some provisions, and he would go to the chapel first. He might be able to sell the shawl to Old Sue, Paul's wife. If he could not, there was at least a chance that she would let him clean the inside of the porridge pot or give him a drink of milk. Now that it was turning cold, free milk would be harder and harder to find. The cows gave less, and the milk kept longer.

Last fall, when their own cow had died, there had been wonderful feasts, and Gloin had gotten winter boots for both of them from Philip in trade for the hide. Now times were lean; somehow they must get a new cow.

He imagined himself with Cope and the abbé (Paul and Gloin and Philip would have turned back in fear long ago) stalking through some remote part of the forest in pursuit of Wat. Unexpectedly they would see him through a gap in the trees, clad all in black and leading a stolen cow. He alone would dash forward; Wat would draw his knife, but he would put his pike point to the wayfarer's throat, and Wat would scream for mercy, and later confess that he had murdered the rightful owner of the cow. Cope and the abbé would agree that it should go to him, since they both had cows already and it was he who overcame Wat. They would tie a noose about Wat's neck and return to the village, with Cope carrying his pike for him while he led the cow with his right hand and Wat with his left.

He swallowed. The salty cheese he had eaten that night had made him thirsty. Regretfully he threw off his warm coverings, thrust his feet into his boots, and went outside to get a drink from the stream. The moon was high now. He swung his arms in the wan light and drained the wooden pannikin four times before his thirst was satisfied.

For some reason, after downing the cold water he felt unwilling to return to bed. The hour or so of rest—alternately dozing and waking, dreaming and daydreaming—had removed the worst of his fatigue, and the exciting events of the evening were stirring in his memory. He recited parts of the abbé's speech as he strolled out to the dying fire in front of the cobbler's. On the black bulk of the Mountain, looming over the Broom and Barrel, no spark showed.

When nights were warmer, he and Josellen often left their beds and met behind the inn to gossip or, more rarely, ride secretly on the chapel path, one behind the other on a horse some pilgrim was boarding at the inn stable. Sometimes, when it was very hot, they even made the long, frightening night walk through the forest to the river to swim, returning exhausted in spite of having rested panting on the riverbank before beginning the trip home.

Occasionally too, when he had been unsuccessful in finding a supper, he had lifted the kitchen latch and stolen apples and turnips from Josellen's father's bins, or found a pork bone or piece of gravy-soaked bread Josellen had left out for him. Tonight he decided to raid the inn even though he was not particularly hungry. There was an excitement in him that made the thought of an apple taken in the dark kitchen and gnawed on the way back to his pallet almost unbearably seductive. He could sense in anticipation the cold juice wetting his cheeks and plashing down his chin as he bit through the peel.

In the stableyard he moved from shadow to shadow in a pattern he had worked out two years before. The dark door creaked back as soon as his hand touched it to feel for the crevice between door and jamb; it had not been latched that night. His hand was pushing it cautiously inward when it swooped away from him; in the dark he saw the white blur of a face before an impetuous soft body bumped against his and he was forced a step back. There was a gasp, then a flurry of excited whispers; then a small hand pressed to his mouth while Josellen pulled him away from the inn.

"What are you doing here, stealing?"

"Josie . . ."

"Listen, do you want to come with me? I'm going to Mother Cloot's."

"Josie!"

"I am. I've never been there, but I know where it is from listening to people talk in our tap; a week ago I went nearly all the way, but I got scared and came back. The abbé's been there, no matter what he says about her. And all the women have, and a lot of shepherds and burners go, too."

While he protested, not so much attempting to dissuade her, or himself, as reserving the right to turn back later, they were already walking among the trees, where in spite of the chill there was a closeness in the air. Above, the atmosphere winced with the approach of the first storm of autumn.

"I want to see if she's there or not. When the abbé saw fire way up on the Mountain and came a-running into our tap and she was gone, you could see right on his face what it was he thought. He figured she was warming her bottom to that fire that very minute. That she'd flown to the gathering on the Mountain in the wink of an eye."

"I don't believe it," Mark said.

"Oh, you don't? Why not?"

Mark tried to recall some of the arguments he had

heard Philip the Cobbler use. At last he said, "Because I never saw anything like that in my whole life."

"Well, how could you? I mean, if she didn't do it while anybody was watching. She'd just be there one time and gone the next—and that's just how it was. Have you ever been this way before?"

"I have in the daytime. Not at night."

"I went farther than this when I tried to see her before, but it's still scary; they say you have to go past Grind-walled. Have you ever been that far up the river?"

He had not, but he attempted to pass it off. "It's just where there used to be a village—only nobody's lived there for a long time."

"Oh, there's been living there, on and off; at least that's what I hear. Only it's been a really long time since it was a town. Sue, the sexton's wife, once told me that in the old time folk in Grindwalled used to see the Good People's boats coming down the current after sunset, going down the river to *Ocean*—that's the big river that goes clear around the world. Do you think things were much differ-ent that long ago?"

When he made no answer, she said half to herself, "Mother Cloot would know."

About them the forest breathed and shivered. They guided themselves much more by the feel of the path be-neath their feet than by the occasional flecks of moonlight leaking down the undersides of the leaves. They had been holding hands as a matter of course since leaving the innyard.

Finally they neared a clearing, and the girl pointed dra-matically. "See! Do you know what that is?"

"It's Miles Cross," Mark said slowly. "I've heard people talking about it, but I always thought it was farther from our village."

It was not a cross. Two flat slabs of stone higher than a tall man had been set into the ground on end, and a third laid on top with a quarter of its length overhanging to either side. Miles Cross stood in the center of an open sward, now moonlit, and behind it Mark could see the rounded rise of a tumulus like an unnaturally smooth and symmetrical hillock. Following the girl, he walked out of the trees and through the rank grass until they stood almost beneath the crosspiece.

"I bet Mother Cloot's up on top of there," Josellen whispered.

"Don't be silly; that's the silliest thing I ever heard of."

The thought frightened him. With an interior vision more vivid than his exterior sight he saw the impassive face of the old woman thrust over the edge as though she were a snake ready to slide off a stone wall.

"Lift me up, Mark. I think if you'll lift me I can grab hold and pull myself high enough to see the top."

Habituated to obeying her, he first made a step of his hands, and when this failed to give her the height she needed, he took her legs and pushed her up while she clung to one of the upright stones to keep her balance. At last with a little cry of triumph she managed to grasp the edge of the capstone.

With Mark raising himself on tiptoe to heave against the soles of her feet, she was able to pull herself up until her head was higher than the surface. To his dismay she continued to climb, leaning forward to throw the weight of her body over the stone and grunting with effort while she kicked the air over his head. He wiped his sweating palms on his tunic and watched as with a rolling motion she twisted herself wholly onto the stone.

"Josie," he called softly. "Josie?"

No answer came. For some reason he could not bring himself to walk through the arch of Miles Cross; but he circled around it trying to see the top. It occurred to him then to climb the tumulus, and he reluctantly did so, finding it both steeper and higher than he had thought it to be. He had to pull himself up the steepest part by the tufts of grass growing from its side, but once on the summit, higher now than Josellen, he could see her in her pale shift walking up and down the top of the cross. When he called to her and waved, she stepped to the edge nearest him and waved in return.

Behind him a cracked voice asked, "Don't you know it's bad luck to walk on a barrow? A barrow's a grave."

Mother Cloot was standing on the tumulus about ten feet to his rear. For an instant he felt certain she had not been there when he had completed his climb and turned around; then he realized that he had been so intent on Josellen that if the old woman had been crouching or sitting he might easily have overlooked her dark figure.

He said, "You're doing it yourself, Mother," and was surprised at how brave he sounded.

"Yes, but I like bad luck." She gave the words a slightly different twist. "You're looking for Josellen, but what's Josellen looking for? There's nothing on Miles Cross—a bare rock—maybe some sticks blown out of the trees in storms." The pauses were little gasps for breath, given not so much as if the old woman were winded by exertion as compelled by the need to draw air past some fluid that clogged her throat.

"She thought you were up there," Mark said. "I don't know why. She thought you had been up on the Mountain tonight at the fire, too."

The old woman cackled. "I was at her own father's—drinkin' his bad ale—'til I 'bout did the springle-ringle down the path. Don't she know that?"

"I don't understand her," Mark said humbly.

More faintly than distance alone accounted for (perhaps because of the rising wind over the forest and the ceaseless fluttering of leaves), Josellen was calling, "Mark, Mark. Who's that with you?"

"It's Mother Cloot," he shouted back. To the old woman he said, "Mother Cloot, wave to her. I don't think she sees you."

She flourished the stick she carried, then taking him by the arm, led him down from the tumulus. She seemed so infirm that he wondered as he helped her scramble down how she had ever climbed it unassisted.

At the foot of the cross she rapped her stick loudly against one of the upright stones to attract the attention of the girl on top, fairly flailing away as though she were beating a horse. When Josellen bent over to see them, clearly a little nervous at standing so close to the edge, the old woman called, "Jump, child. Jump down. It won't hurt you."

Mark could see Josellen was frightened; but she hesitated only a moment before she jumped, her shift billowing about her. She landed with a thump close beside them and pitched forward on her hands and knees.

"Get up now." The old woman prodded her with her staff. "You're not hurt."

Josellen rose stiffly, rubbing her hands together and then on her skirt and knees. "I bruised myself a bit," she said, "but it was wonderful being up there. I felt, you know, really high and noble. Above everything, like a cloud." She looked from Mark's face to Mother Cloot's and back as though to see if either understood what she was trying to express.

"I'll put some ointment on your hurts later, child." The old woman grasped each of them by the hand as she spoke, simultaneously giving her stick to Mark to carry. "You really ought to climb the Mountain at least once in your life, dear, as I did—when I was just a girl myself— you'd enjoy it so."

As they started to walk together, Mark was conscious that Mother Cloot was not only much shorter than he, but even shorter than Josellen. To his dismay she led them straight through the arch of the cross so that for a few seconds they were in inky darkness with the moonlight before them and behind.

She turned them sharply when they came from under it, until they were walking nearly parallel to the long line of the tumulus. It looked like a wall, and Mark had the feeling that it served to shelter something that stalked them from the other side. Going into the darkness under the trees again was comforting after that sensation of naked exposure.

"You children," Mother Cloot said, "shouldn't be running about in the wood like this. Wolves—all kinds of nasty things—are out. All boys are stupid, but you ought to know better, Josellen."

"We've gone out before and nothing ever got us," Josellen said. She was giggling with excitement.

"And if something had gotten you, you wouldn't be here—solid and warm—pink—talking to me." Mother Cloot cleared her throat, a noise like water pouring out on the ground, and spat. "You'd be inside there"—she gestured back in the direction of the tumulus—"talking to the Barrow Man—maybe."

"You mean Mark and me'd be ghosts? Who's the Barrow Man?"

"Whatever you want to call it, dear. Barrow Man's him that's buried back there in the barrow—the man Mark here stepped on the face of. Now me, nothing that's in these woods would touch—know I'd make 'em sick to eat of me." Mother Cloot looked at Mark as she spoke. "Had bears and things come right up and smell of me—turn and walk off. Know that?"

"Holy people get along with wild animals too," Mark said. He was thinking of one of the abbé's most frightening sermons, in which children who mocked a prophet were eaten by the animal that had refused Mother Cloot.

"Oh, that's easy." The old woman spat again, the saliva nearly hitting Mark's foot this time. "Anybody can get along with them that loves them—animals most never harms them. It's doing the one without the other that's hard. Who wants to love a bear? Do you?"

Mark thought of the bear he had seen at the baiting at last year's fair and decided he did not.

"Stink," Mother Cloot said forcefully. "Full of fleas and ticks, and got flies 'round their eyes when they sleeps. And let me tell you this—once let one in the house, he's the master. A person can't actually love anything stronger than herself"—she gave one of her gasps—"unless it's like a horse—too stupid to do anything but what it's told."

Mark wanted to object, but could think of nothing to say.

"And when you meet a bear, you just try to love it real quick, before it can get to you—think that's easy?"

Josellen said, "You'd have to love it to start with, before you ever saw it."

"Don't you try, dear. You love a pony if you like—not a bear—too rough. The loving you give before they arrive isn't appreciated."

She had been leaning more and more heavily on Mark's arm as she spoke, until he could scarcely keep his balance. Now she said, "Sit down here a bit, children. I'm too tired, almost, to walk."

The forest earth was damp and cold, but Mother Cloot seemed to throw herself squarely down on it, as nearly as Mark could see in the shadows. He himself squatted on his heels, and Josellen felt about with her hands until she found a tree root that thrust up a bow of wood from the soil.

"You children are going to spend the night with me, aren't you?" Mother Cloot asked. "Can't be wandering the wood all night."

"We started out to see you," Josellen told her, "but we have to get back to our beds before anyone in the village gets up. Really, I guess since we've seen you there's no reason to go all the way to your house."

Mark thought Josellen was becoming a trifle frightened.

"Like Barrow Man, eh? Have to be in your bed come sunup." Mother Cloot seemed to be chewing something vigorously as she spoke, and Mark had the impression that it was something she had taken from the bosom of her gown a moment before. "Know he has a bed in there? Real one. I don't mean just a grave like most."

"No, I didn't. Have you been inside?"

"Honest wooden bed, but the posts are X's. Crossed over, like, at each end, and animal heads—werefoxes all red and gold they was once—cut into 'em. Mark, dear, I'm that tired I'll never get to my own bed tonight. Would you take me up?"

He did not at first understand what she meant, but she rose (rather spryly, he thought) and before he could stand, clambered onto his shoulders; not pig-a-back, but with her legs fairly about his neck on either side and her belt buckle chafing the back of his head. He did not like it at all—her gown had a dirty, musty smell—but he was too young to feel he could order her to get down. She drummed her heels against his ribs, not humorously or even taunt-ingly, but in a natural way, as though she were accustomed to doing it.

"Come, children. Barrow Man don't like moonlight, even, but the moon'll be down soon now—have to get away from his garden."

At least she was light to carry, Mark reflected. Under the filthy bundle of clothes her body must be starved down to the last shreds of flesh. Wryly he consoled himself with the thought that he would have collapsed beneath her were she only half the weight of Philip's wife. As it was, she was like a scarecrow come to life, held up by light, hard sticks that pressed through her skin wherever they touched him.

"Hear the river?" the old woman said when no one had spoken for several minutes.

Mark and Josellen both said, "No."

"Well, I hear it, and you soon will too. Path goes right

by for a way. Sliding over mud, 'round rushes and willow roots, the river water. There's—swords in that water, boy." She rapped Mark on the head with her knuckles as if to make certain he was paying attention. "You hand me my stick up—want to fend some of these twigs off—and I'll tell you about 'em."

He did as she asked, interested in spite of himself.

"Well now," she said, and Mark sensed in the shifting of her weight the way she was flourishing her staff in front of her face, "used to be a town up the bank here. Where you come from isn't anything—to compare with what *it* was. Big log houses—stone houses." She spat. "People there didn't farm 'cept for little bits of gardening. Didn't herd sheep or pigs neither, nor burn charcoal to sell, but they were richer than people now—just hunted the wood and fished the river."

"How did they get rich then?" Josellen asked.

"They knew where gold was—on the Mountain, and they knew how to keep what they gained. That's the art your folk have forgotten, child."

Josellen exclaimed, "This is it now, isn't it?"

The trees had been thinning for the last hundred yards, and the oaks and maples were giving place to willows that were not the formal Oriental willows of gardens. Murmurous thickets grew in soil that was increasingly sandy beneath Mark's feet, and now he could hear the soft flowing of the river water.

"Right there." Mother Cloot pointed with her stick, and where the trees were thin Mark could see the place she indicated under faded moonlight. "There's where the old ones lived—lived when nobody inside a thousand miles ever heard of Moses or Jesus or any of that."

A point of land, higher than the rest and stony, jutted out into the river here, with a little stream trickling along the far side and broadening into a miniature bay where it met the river. Long ago there had been a palisade of upright stakes surrounding the whole of the point on the water side as well as the land, and extending across the widening stream to trace its far bank for fifty ells before crossing again at the point where the stream narrowed. Their path entered the enclosure through a break in the rotted stubs, wandered errantly through what had been a village, then left at this narrow spot.

"That's the *grind*, there where the wall went through the water," Josellen said, pointing. She sounded proud of her knowledge. "That's why they called it Grindwalled, isn't it, Mother?"

"Isn't what the folk who dwelt here called it." As they passed through the break in the palisade, the old woman spoke softly, two words quite unknown to Mark, and he felt that she had saluted an unseen sentry. The path dodged this way and that through the rounded hummocks that had once been buildings. He could form only the poorest idea of what the plan of the village had been, but dark-mouthed burrows in some of these heaps made him think of what Josellen had said earlier—of someone still living here—and he shuddered.

"You could well shake," Mother Cloot said above him, "if those that once walked here were still in flesh—or if I weren't with you. Had long knives, they did, and short tempers. The swords in the river are ones they threw in— enemies' blades with gold hilts and blue and green stones. Sent 'em in to guard the fords."

"They'd be rusted away by now," Mark said.

Mother Cloot shook her head so violently that Mark felt she was about to fall from his shoulders. "Bronze," she said. "Blades like big leaves—turned green is all. I've seen 'em."

"Do I have to wade through this water?"

"Sure. Folk used to hop across on those stumps—that's why the track runs here, but they're too rotten now. Turn under you."

"All right," Mark said wearily. "Josellen, I'll set Mother Cloot on the far side, then come back for you."

The creek bottom was treacherous, and at the deepest point the icy water came almost to his armpits. When he returned for the girl, he said softly, "Josie, let's go home. We can leave her there and just run off." But Josellen shook her head.

She was considerably heavier than the old woman, and he carried her in his arms instead of on his shoulders, lifting her to keep her clear of the water. Until he had put Mother Cloot down, he had not realized how tired his shoulders were; when Josellen was on dry ground once more, he flexed them, feeling the ache in his muscles. Seeing him, the old woman said, "I can walk for the rest of it, child," in a tone that was almost kind, and he warmed to her a bit. The night was now nearly half spent, and the desire for a bed, quiet, and sleep had come rushing down on him.

She—and the path—led them away from the river now; back among the big forest trees. Somewhere they must have left the main way, for the path was even narrower and fainter than it had been through Grindwalled. "Home, home," Mother Cloot said cheerfully.

Mark looked around, but could see no cottage.

Nearly dancing with delight at their surprise, Mother

Cloot pointed upward with her staff, and staring up into the blackness Mark became aware that a dark mass hung over the trail above them. Beams, or at least poles, had been run between four great oaks, two on each side of the path. They formed a square, with an X in the middle for support of the center of the floor. The trunks of saplings had been laid across this framework and a hut built on top.

Looking at this platform house and at the great trees with gnarled roots that supported it, Mark found himself remembering (in that half-dreaming way the old memories had of coming back when he was tired) his dead mother telling stories before the fire when they lived behind the manor house at Pyedmeadows. There had been a tale about a witch who lived in a house built on four chicken legs; and now, shivering in the dark, sensing the roots of the oaks spread like toes, he knew he was standing beneath the original of that story.

"Come up, Mark," Mother Cloot's voice called. "Ladder's over here."

It was a rope ladder with wooden rungs, his fingers told him. He climbed slowly, aware that he should not, but equally aware of the impossibility of spending the remainder of the night in the forest below. Besides, Josellen was going, already climbing ahead of him.

A box of sand had been set in the center of the hut, and a fire smoldered there. It gave a faint red light to the interior. "Plenty of room for all," Mother Cloot said. She seemed in a jovial mood now, and Mark was reminded of Gloin's merriment when he had drunk ale without eating.

In a corner someone moved, and grunted sleepily.

"Don't bother yourself, Wat," Mother Cloot said. "It's just some children come to spend the night."

4

AFTERWARD, IT SEEMED to Mark that he had lain awake all night, touching the hilt of the knife in his stocking and drawing his hand away again. It was not that he felt any scruple against taking life; he wanted, ardently, passionately, to kill Wat. Or rather, he wanted *to have killed Wat*. But in imagination he watched himself drop the knife in his haste, deal only a flesh wound, find Wat awake after all. He was bothered, too, by memories of the abbé's sermons in which such things were called cowardly. He could not understand why, if it were cowardly, he, who had never thought himself a coward, should be so frightened.

After a time Josellen rolled over to press her back against him for warmth. He wrapped his arms around her, apparently to her satisfaction since she went soundly back to sleep. He was cold himself, and desperately lonely in the problem of Wat. Rain rattled against the walls of the hut and came down the smoke hole in the center of the conical roof, making the fire splutter.

*   *   *

Unexpectedly the smoke hole had grown light, and a handsome man in black was shaking him by the shoulder and grinning with ivory teeth. "Come down to the river with me," Wat said, "and we'll get the old hag some water."

Numbly, stiff with cold, Mark got up. Outside he saw that the rain had stopped and the wayfarer had been busy already. The little fire in the hut had been allowed to go out, but a new one blazed on the ground below. Wat let him warm himself by it for a few minutes before they took up buckets and started down the path to the river.

"You and the girl stay with Mother Cloot often?" Wat asked casually.

The question took Mark by surprise. "I never have before at all," he managed to say at last. Now that he was away from the fire, his teeth were chattering again. "Josellen says she hasn't either, but I'm not sure that's true." Greatly daring, but conscious that the answer might be of value in the future, he added, "Do you?"

Wat laughed outright, throwing back his head and barking his merriment in a way that was both pleasant and a shade savage. He was tall, a well-set-up man with high cheekbones, black hair, and bright blue eyes. His rusty, dark clothing reminded Mark somehow of the abbé, though Wat wore hose instead of the abbé's habit. "Not I! I've a hundred dozen places to sleep more comfortable than her bird nest. Quicker to get out of when you hear someone coming, too."

"You didn't hear us coming," Mark ventured.

"Yes, I did, half in my sleep. I heard the old woman talking to you too, though, and knew from the sound of her that it was all right. She's a good old thing, Mother

Cloot is, I suppose, but mad as a March hare by moonlight if you ask me. I always bring her a bit of mutton or venison when I come by and carry her up some water if I've the time, so she's always glad to see me."

"Everyone's afraid of her in our village."

"You're from the village? You'd be the weaver's boy, then."

"I'm his 'prentice." Mark discovered that he was most unwilling that Wat should think him Gloin's son.

"And you're one of that dread band enlisted against me." Wat was smiling as he looked over his shoulder to say this, but Mark was a little frightened nonetheless.

"Do you know about it?" he asked diplomatically.

"Gil told me. He'd got the idea earlier—from talking to that surly old bone-miner Paul—that something of the sort was intended, so I sent him into the village last night. Mother Cloot's was a good place to meet; at least there's usually a fire to sit around."

As he tried to dip up the icy, rushing water without sliding down the bank into it, Mark reflected that the old woman must have heard Wat talking to the charcoal burner—that was "Gil," obviously—and decided to see the fun herself. He was silent all the way back to the fire, though Wat whistled merrily in a way that indicated he was amused at carrying water in the company of one of the village militia.

When Josellen came down, they were toasting gobbets from the unidentifiable haunch-of-something Wat had brought. She looked pale and sleepy and was quieter than Mark had ever seen her before. He cut her a green stick so that she could roast herself some breakfast, feeling adult and protective as he did it, perhaps partly because she was seeing him on such easy terms with the famous outlaw.

"You know," Wat remarked as they ate, "having the two of you here is going to be awfully helpful. Would either of you consider going by St. Agnes' and leaving a message with the pastor?"

Both nodded in bewilderment.

Wat seemed to consider a moment. "In that case it had better be you, Josellen. That's your name, isn't it? I believe the boy mentioned it."

Josellen said it was.

"Well, Josie, from what I hear your family's not very popular with the abbé's little band of heroes, and if I sent Mark, they might decide that it was worth a wench one way or the other to get rid of me."

"You mean Mark is going to have to stay here with you?"

"Yes." Wat nodded solemnly. "And if there's any treachery, you may tell them, Mark will have his ears cut off, and other things as well."

"If you want to talk to the head of the militia," Mark put in, "it's Philip, not the abbé."

Wat shook his head. "You go by the chapel, Josie," he said, "and nowhere else but home. Now here's what I want you to tell the abbé—"

A weak voice from the treehouse called. "Wat . . . Wat . . ." and the wayfarer looked up in irritation. "What's the matter up there?" he asked. The reply was too weak to be understood. Wat shouted, "We'll fetch you down in a minute," then continued his instructions to Josellen.

"You tell the abbé I'll meet with him and all his militia to make arrangements for my leaving. Make it at sun-

set in your father's tap. Tell them no one is to bring
weapons and that Mark will suffer for it if I don't like the
catering." He gestured toward the path. "Be away now."

As the girl left, Wat added to Mark in a low voice,
"Tender bit, that. I hope you appreciate her; you'll not find
much better."

Mark did not know what to reply. He would have said
anything to make himself a man in Wat's eyes, but he was
painfully conscious that anything he might say would be
treated as a joke. Since some reply seemed expected, he at
last mumbled, "Well, I don't know. I mean, I've never had
anything to compare her to."

Wat roared with laughter, blotting out the feeble mew-
ings from the treehouse. When he had gotten his breath
again, he slapped Mark on the shoulder and said, "You'll
do. Listen now: go up in the magpie's nest there and fetch
her down for me. And don't pay too much mind to what
I said about slicing off ears. I had to put a bit of a chill into
your girl so she'd do the same to that ditch priest and his
flagon knights."

Mark felt somewhat relieved as he climbed the ladder
to Mother Cloot's hovel again.

The old woman lay close by the dead fire, wrapped in
rags she apparently kept as bedding for herself. She seemed
to try to speak as Mark came in, but no intelligible words
resulted. Her eyes rolled and her lips trembled convulsively, and a thin string of spittle ran down her cheek.
Mark picked her up as carefully as he could, finding her
lighter than he remembered, and laid her across his shoulders so that he could negotiate the ladder. When he
reached the bottom, Wat produced a horn flask from a

pocket of his jacket. The contents gave a rich aroma to the forest air and made the old woman choke and sputter.

"Heart of wine," Wat said proudly. "Take good Burgundy in a leathern bottle and leave it out on the coldest night of winter; in the morning pour this off and throw away the bottle and the ice—if the church used this at mass, they'd rule the world."

"It must be expensive," Mark said. To him wine itself represented almost unapproachable luxury. "Is she going to die?"

"Not her! I've seen her worse than this; life'll come when the sun strikes her—that always brings life of one sort or another. If muscles don't move, maggots do." Wat pulled a soft doeskin bag from the front of the old woman's gown and tossed it to Mark. "Hang this on a limb somewhere so she can't kill herself with it until she's strong enough to die." Mark did as he was told, noticing the bag had a peculiar herbal smell. After a time Mother Cloot made a weak gesture toward one of the water buckets, and they held it up between them for her to sip from.

"Wait here a moment," Wat said. "Then we've got to move along. I want to collect Gil before the congress of catch-thieves." He disappeared into the trees, and returned carrying a bow and wearing a quiver and a long sword in a black leather scabbard.

Mark said, "You'll be all right," to Mother Cloot in a voice he tried to make reassuring. She ignored him, or rather seemed not to have heard him. Her eyes were fixed on Wat's fire, as if seeing there something terrible and fascinating.

Wat said, "I'll lead the way. If you have trouble keeping up, yell," and he set a fast pace.

When they were well away from the fire, Mark asked, "Is she really a witch?"

"Of course."

Somehow this did not seem a satisfactory answer. After a time Mark asked, "How do you know?" and Wat was irritated enough to halt his long strides to reply.

"Listen, if there's such a thing as a witch, she's one; and if there's no such thing, there's no reason for having the word."

"If she's a witch, she's evil," Mark persisted. "Why did you help her?"

Contemptuously Wat said, "Because I'm evil too." He was walking again and did not bother to look over his shoulder to make the reply. "Besides, she'd make a ghastly ghost."

"Well, can she put a candle of dead man's fat into the straw of a broom and ride it through the air as long as the candle burns?"

"Can you? Have you ever tried?"

"You know what I mean." Mark felt that Wat was making fun of him now.

"Better than you do yourself. You mean can she do miracles like St. Agnes or St. Hubert—only miracles that are bad. The sort you and I would like to do. Don't you?"

"I suppose so."

"Certainly you do. You've often thought while you were hearing the gospel in church that curing the sick and bringing back the dead would be fun—especially if there were plenty of people to watch and admire you—but you'd really rather be able to kill the people you don't like in some mysterious, impressive way. So have I. How old are you, Mark?"

"Fourteen."

"Well, that's a good age, and with a little help you could stop right there." Wat drew his long dagger as he said this, and without looking back, began to run his thumb up and down the edge as though he were going to carve a roast.

"I didn't mean any harm," Mark protested.

"Ah, that's the trouble. To get along the way old Cloot does, you have to." When Wat turned to face Mark again, he sheathed the blade, his eyes glittering. "You see, the hag really can do things, but if you wanted to do them too, you'd have to be the way she is—not just bad some of the times, but bad all the time. I've never been able to make the effort myself; I've cut a lot of throats, but every once in a while my sense of fun comes creeping in."

"If she really can"—Mark saw vistas of limitless power—"why doesn't she just take charge of everything? If I were her—"

"You'd live in a crystal castle on a golden hill with fifty princesses to wait on you."

"I suppose so."

"But she wouldn't. She'd feed the princesses to the pigs, then paint the pigs with poison. Then she'd smash your castle and sink the hill in a swamp. You see, she *has* taken over everything she could. You don't see it because what she took she destroyed. She was mistress of a manor farm once, with hired shepherds and drovers to care for her stock."

Mark said, "It seems there isn't much good in being bad after all," not realizing that he had made a feeble witticism until he had finished the sentence.

"People are afraid of her, and she enjoys that. Also, she

really does get to revenge herself on the people she doesn't like—at least, pretty often."

"I don't suppose she likes anyone, if she's as bad as you say."

Wat laughed at that, and Mark wondered at the wild sound his laughter held. "I don't suppose she does, but at least she hates some more than others. A person like myself gets better use out of his misbehavior. It's a sword in my hand to cut with when I want and sheath when I want. . . ." As he said the last word, Wat drew his sword and whirled to touch the point to Mark's chest, all in one beautiful, practiced motion. For an instant Mark was certain that Wat was ready to kill him, or would be were there anyone watching to applaud.

A moment later Wat smiled and said calmly, "It's a good blade. Like to hold it?"

As Mark felt the sharpness of the blade and bent it gingerly in the pretense of being able to judge the temper, Wat continued, "You said a while ago that the heart of wine must be costly. It isn't for me; I steal it. I took that sword from a man who wasn't fit to hold it, and I take other things in the same way: horses, clothes, women, coin. But I keep the good things I take—at least for as long as I want them. And I enjoy them. The man who bought that sword probably hated it because it cost him a sack of gold; I love it because it reminds me of a victory."

5

HEY HAD TO go a long way to reach the charcoal burners' camp, and most of it was uphill. The flanks of the Mountain were covered with a forest as dense as that at its foot for nearly a quarter of its elevation; through this forest Wat and Mark climbed until the sun was well overhead. As they progressed, Wat, who had been so casual and confident in the lowlands, became silent and watchful. Mark himself felt uprooted, separated from his bed in Gloin's webstery not only by miles and hours but by all the events that had taken place since he left it to steal an apple. He felt certain Gloin would not take him back if he knew a fraction of what had happened. He was almost equally sure that he could not return even if he and Gloin both wished it. A person (he could not call himself a man and would not call himself a boy) who had slept at Mother Cloot's and walked through half the forest with Wat could not, surely, resume even the life of a weaver, much less that of an apprentice.

The smell of the smoke intruded on their senses long

before they sighted the camp. Charcoal burners were a necessary infraction of the forest law that in theory ruled everyone who dwelt inside the "fence"—the legal boundary that separated the forest from the world of fiefs and farms—and as such they ranked about halfway between tinkers and gypsies. Supposedly they felled no living trees, but made their product out of windfalls and blight-stricken trunks. In practice, since the legal method would have been prohibitively laborious, forcing them to drag the fallen wood for miles, they cut everything of size in each area they settled, keeping far enough from the "fences" that they were not often molested.

Their camp was two hide tents and a leafy hut built of the lop-and-top that lay everywhere about. In front of the tents three kilns were in various stages of burning, judging from the degree to which each had fallen in—each kiln being simply a smoldering rick of wood over which earth had been heaped in such a way as to half smother the fire without extinguishing it. The result, less ashes and burnt earth, would be charcoal. Several nearly naked children were playing upwind of the kilns.

Remaining in the shade of the last unfelled trees in the circle about the camp, Wat shouted for Gil, and Mark sensed that he did not want to walk into the open. A woman somewhere bawled the same name, and this produced an unintelligible cry from the trees higher up the slope. It occurred to Mark that the burners probably preferred to cut there, since they could then slide the logs downhill.

"He'll be along," the woman called.

Wat seated himself on a stump without relaxing. "I've told you the good part of my life already, Mark," he said.

"Now I'll tell you the bad. It's that you have to trust some-one, but you can't trust anyone. Not when you've got a price on your head. Have you ever seen a charcoal camp? Go have a look around. If there's any about who shouldn't be, the sight of a stranger may bring them out."

Mark *had* seen such camps before, but only rarely, the last when he had been a good deal younger. He stared at the kilns, tents, and bower with considerable interest. Then he noticed a blackened object like a post standing in the center of the camp and remembered Gil's remark about having a statue of the Virgin. It was hard to tell what the postlike thing was, and he went over to look at it. The naked children had stopped their play to stare at him with round eyes. He felt the warmth of sunlight on his back.

The image was three-quarters life size, old and smoke-blacked and battered looking. It depicted what might have been either a woman or a young man, noseless now, whose hair was covered with a sort of angular headdress of folded cloth. The face was impassive, and it seemed to Mark that the eyes had originally been closed. They were now painted (the entire figure gave evidence of having been painted in various ways at various times) with pupilless blue circles that gave an impression of blindness.

Some tiny sound told Mark that Wat was standing be-side and just behind him. Without looking back he asked, "Is it Mary?"

"I suppose so." Wat sounded bored now. "I've always had a notion she was originally someone else, perhaps Freyr or Freya; but there's no question but that she's Mary now—at least to visitors."

Mark had never heard of Freyr or Freya and was not sufficiently sophisticated to grasp the idea of a statue's changing identities. "Well, which is it really," he asked impatiently, "Mary or Freya?"

"The charcoal burners call it The Unwed One," Wat said, "and I suppose that could be either. What makes you so certain the two are different? Perhaps both the names, all the names, are for the same thing—Freya yesterday, Mary today, something else after we're gone."

"Because Mary was a real, living person," Mark said stoutly, "and either something's made to be a picture of her or it isn't."

"Good cess," a voice called, and Mark turned to see the one-eyed charcoal burner who had been at the Broom and Barrel the previous evening. He was walking bandy-legged across the clearing toward them, holding his broadax in one hand while he waved the other.

"Good morrow, Gil," Wat called politely. "Did you get home in time to get any sleep last night?"

"Oh, I'm fine and fit," the charcoal burner said complacently, then added to Mark, "Don't I know you, lad? Seems there was more of Wat's friends about yesterday than I knew."

"Not Mark," the wayfarer said easily. "He's a bold clutch-knave—but I hope to make better of him in time." More seriously he asked, "And how are our friends uphill?"

"Still there; I've set a boy to watch them. It's hard, though, to hold the rest here. Everyone wanted to cut no more and move down to the bottoms as soon as what we have's burnt."

"I doubt they'll give you any trouble; they want something more than burners."

"Aye," Gil admitted glumly, "but if they don't get such, they won't go home with nothing to show. We'll take our chances, though. How's to something to bite and swallow?"

They followed Gil to the bower, where a smudged girl brought them bread and cold mutton and home-brewed ale, dark and unpleasantly sweet.

"Now then," Gil asked when they had refreshed themselves, "you've something you want of me?"

"Only that you make a bit of a journey with us. Down to the village, then out upon the highway, it may be."

Gil looked uninterested. "The usual terms? Someone's got to stay here at the camp sometimes to look after the folk, you know."

"A third of all I get."

The charcoal burner's mouth pursed as if he were whistling, though no sound came. "There's many a one would follow you for less than that; I could have some to follow *me* for a bit of that share, for that matter."

"I want you. None of the rest of your woodchoppers will stick when there's trouble. Also for that money, could you find something for the boy here? It would be best if he didn't wander the wood with just his empty hands."

"Can you hit with a bow, lad?" Gil seemed doubtful.

Mark shook his head. The idea of accepting a weapon from these people carried a connotation of changed loyalty that disturbed him. Gil looked thoughtful for a moment, then left the leafy shanty.

In a few minutes he was back, carrying a light, short-handled hatchet in the same hand as his broadax, and with a leather bundle like a rucksack slung over one shoulder. Helplessly Mark accepted the hatchet.

As he had before, Wat led the way, seeming quite careless of Mark and his own unprotected back. Gil walked beside Mark where the track was wide enough to permit it, and once when Wat had gotten a good way ahead, he whispered, "He wants you to try to kill him with that half-ax. Don't." Mark nodded, not certain he understood.

They took a different path from the one Wat and Mark had followed, and after walking swiftly for half an hour, reached the bank of a rushing stream, the infant beginning of the river at the Mountain's foot.

When he unfolded it on a grassy spot, Gil's leather bundle proved to be a great bag of thin-scraped hides sewn together with almost invisibly small stitching. While Mark watched in wonder, Gil cut saplings and fashioned a wicker framework, working with astonishing speed, lashing the joints with smaller, pliant twigs. When he had laced the bag over the frame, he could lift the whole affair easily, ungainly as it was. Last of all he cut himself a pole about seven feet long.

"You jump in first," he told Mark when the frail-looking craft was in the water. "Wat'll come after, and I'll shove us off."

Mark did as he was told, expecting the hide boat to tip over at once; but Wat's weight pushed it lower in the water, until the bottom was scraping lightly on the pebbles of the stream bed. Holding the boat by an edge, Gil laid his pole across it, then waded out until they were again floating free. With an agile hop he managed to get in himself without upsetting them.

"How will you get back up here?" Mark asked. Clearly the bag boat could not be poled up against the current.

"Throw away the sticks and carry up the skin," the charcoal burner replied cheerfully. "That's how we always do."

The pole trailed out behind them, preventing the little coracle from spinning in the current; but still it swung from side to side in every eddy and pitched alarmingly wherever sunken rocks caused upshoots and undertows. The trees on the banks seemed not so much to fly past as to be thrown past, skipping and reeling. The seams in the hide cover leaked in spots, and from time to time they shipped water—this ranging from a fine spray to a cold half-bucketful in the course of a particularly dangerous roll. Mark bailed with his hands as well as he could, terrified all the while that his movements might somehow interfere with Gil's.

Unexpectedly the wild motion ceased. They were in shallows again; Gil tossed his pole ashore and leaped out to drag them closer to the bank. Wat climbed out with Mark following gingerly, letting Gil pull the boat completely out of the water and upend it to pour out the bilge. There was a roaring louder than the swift flood of the stream; Mark knew it must indicate rapids even Gil thought too turbulent to shoot. He helped the charcoal burner carry the boat down a twisting path to the foot of them, Wat stalking grandly ahead.

The second stage was much like the first, except that Mark had some idea now of what to expect, and the current was not quite so swift. There was another portage, this time around a low falls, before they reached the broader, relatively tranquil river with which Mark was familiar. Here all fear—of the water at least—left him, and he began to enjoy the trip.

They traveled just as fast as a floating log and no faster, Gil using his stick only to fend off snags and keep them in the center of the current. Here was what Mark, living in and speaking with the outlook of the village, had been accustomed to call the upper river. The water was green rather than clear or foam-scudded as it had been above the falls; the banks were lined with trees and undercut in many places, places where bass and pike would lurk. They were still too near the Mountain for him to recognize land-marks—there was no spot here where he had caught a big fish or swum with Josellen—but it was again the river to which he was accustomed, bringing back to his thoughts with new urgency Gloin and Philip and the abbé and Josellen's father. Half an hour later Gil steered for the shallows, and with a start Mark recognized the high point of Grindwalled and the row of rotting piles across the mouth of the creek there.

Ahead was a narrow space where several of the stumps had been removed or had decayed completely; Gil put the coracle through this gap, though with so little room to ei-ther side that Mark felt certain they would wedge, and landed them close to the place where Mark had waded across with Mother Cloot on his shoulders. They were no sooner out of the boat than Gil stripped the wicker frame free of the leather, and with a wide swing of his short, brawny arm sent it spinning out to the center of the river again. The leather covering he wiped with great care, folded, and carried with him while they ascended to the site of the ruined town.

"Will we be going by Miles Cross?" Mark asked. Even in the light of afternoon he had no desire to visit that enigmatic structure again.

Wat shook his head. "I want to swing around farther to the east. Come on." He took Mark by the arm. "Gil doesn't like anyone to see where he caches his boat skin."

The ruined buildings of Grindwalled showed far less of

their original shapes and structures than Mark had imagined the night before. Mere grassy mounds, they did not display the regularity of form, much less the size, of the tumulus behind Miles Cross. Still, he was glad to leave them. When they were beyond Gil's hearing, Wat asked softly, "What was it Gil said to you when we were going to get the boat?" He seemed to expect a frank answer.

Mark said carefully, "He told me it would be very dangerous for me even to think of harming you."

Wat appeared to relax a little. "They're very proud of me, you know," he said. "They got up the money bit by little to send me to the Benedictines, and of course they were disappointed when I left. I've made it up to them though, I think."

"Were you a monk?" Mark was surprised, off his guard.

"Oh no." The wayfarer laughed deprecatingly. "I thought everyone knew. Only a student. I was supposed to become a priest, of course, but there were difficulties. Technically I suppose I still hold minor orders."

"I'd wondered. You always seem so, you know, gentlemanlike."

Wat bowed in an exaggerated way Mark failed to recognize as a burlesque of a courtier. "Gil's coming. Let's be off."

Instead of turning in the direction of the cross, he led them down a path that paralleled the river, and he seemed to become gayer as he walked, whistling tunes and birdcalls under his breath and occasionally singing snatches of country ballads. Mark thought that earlier he might have been afraid Gil was planning to betray him, but now felt reassured. It was clear, too, that both Wat and Gil were concerned about someone or something higher up the

Mountain. Wat, at least, was happy to be away in the lowlands again, though perhaps Gil felt uneasy about the band of burners left without his leadership. The memory of the tiny scarlet point of light he had seen over the rooftree of the inn returned to Mark. It must have been very high, nearly to the ice line, to have been visible where it was. He debated with himself whether to ask Wat about it and decided to keep silent.

After a time Wat left the river's marge and began, so it seemed to Mark, to cut from path to path and sometimes to use no trail at all. He and Gil followed a few paces behind. Twice they went through thickets where, at some time past, small fires had been built in the shelter of the crowding leaves and someone had trampled flat a spot large enough for a man to lie down in. Following the thought these places suggested, Mark asked Gil boldly, "Where does Wat stay in the winter? When it's snowing and truly cold?"

"Sometimes with the shepherds, or with us charcoal burners," Gil answered frankly. "He pays well enough and never lingers long."

"You never know where I'll be, Mark." They had overtaken Wat. "In the summer I usually camp up on the Mountain near the timberline. It's cool, and I can see anyone coming a long way off. Of course"—he looked over his shoulder at Mark—"I have to come down here on business a lot, and inquisitive people should remember that my knife and I may be closer than they think."

Mark kept silent after this, and since Gil seemed to feel no inclination to talk, for a time they moved along quietly save for Wat's low whistling. There was no wind, and the trees about them shared their silence. Mark noticed that even the foliage this far down the Mountain had begun to turn.

He had lost all sense of direction since leaving the river and was startled when he recognized the path they were about to strike. It was an extension of the pilgrims' path from village to chapel, running from the shrine to the riverbank trail. Wat turned up it, striding along energetically; then, after rounding the first bend, he stopped abruptly and looked back toward Gil—as if in some surprise. Mark pushed forward curiously. A dead man was hanging head down from a limb over the path.

His body was bent back like a bow, with the face pressed in the mud while the feet dangled from the limb; his arms were outspread. He looked as though he might have been laid face down at just that spot until his ankles were pulled up by someone who had carried a rope into the tree. A long, narrow wound at the back of his head was crusted with earth, and fresh earth clung to his clothes.

Mark ran forward and gently shifted the dead man's head until he could see the face. "It's Paul," he called back. "Old Paul the Sexton."

Wat nodded solemnly. "I thought it was," he said.

Coming forward, he examined the wound in the dead man's head. "I would say he was struck from behind with an ax. It might conceivably have been a broadsword or a two-hander, but I think an ax is most probable."

"I saw him." Mark knit his brows. "I saw him when we buried the peddler. . . ." Recalling what was supposed to have happened to the peddler, he stopped in confusion.

"The peddler I got the other day on the highroad?" Wat asked. "Oh, yes," he added, seeing Mark's look of surprise, "I put my second-best shaft in his neck. I don't like the breed—nasty, whining creatures that cry and say you're taking their last farthing when they've half a dozen of gold in one shoe and a thousand more, like as not, in the mattress at home. But"—he laid his right hand against his chest—"I swear to you 'pon my honor—and I never break *that* oath, do I, Gil?—that I didn't kill your friend Paul here. No mea culpa."

"He didn't come to the meeting," Mark said, "and that wasn't like him. He was very bitter about the pilgrims not coming to the shrine anymore." He was trying to untie the knot that held Paul's feet, but his fingers could not loosen it; at last he drew the knife from his stocking top and cut the rope.

"Hurt his pride, no doubt," Wat said, "and his purse too. Being sexton and sacristan both, he must have had some nice opportunities to pick up tips back in the old palmy days—I refer to the palms borne by the pilgrims."

Mark pulled the sexton's body to the side of the path and looked around for something to put over his face, but found nothing.

"Go through his pockets," Wat suggested helpfully. "He might have a handkerchief; besides, you're certainly entitled to keep anything you find."

Shuddering, Mark did so, but it seemed another hand had been there before his. Paul's pockets held nothing whatsoever.

"Then lay a broad maple leaf over his face," Wat instructed him, "and weigh it with a stone. That's good enough for a forest man."

As they walked away, Mark said, "You'd think whoever killed a good man like him would want to hide it instead of hanging him up where he's sure to be found."

"Oh, they did. You'd find a shallow grave about some-where if you went looking, I'm sure." Wat looked thought-ful. "Didn't you see the dirt on him? Someone dug him up later—that would be today, since he seems to have been under the mold during the rain last night. And there're not enough that use this path for him to be found right away."

"We're not far from his house," Mark said despon-dently. "I suppose I ought to tell his wife."

"No, we're not far, and that suggests a favor I'd like to have you do for Gil and me. I want you to go to the house—I assume the sexton's wife will still be there, as you say—and see what you can discover about the abbé's plans for this evening. That bouncy little redhead of yours should have gotten to him sometime before noon, and a woman that keeps house for him ought to know everything about it by now. All I want is to make certain there's no trap being laid; my own offer was fair and clear, you know. You'll do it for me?"

Mark nodded. They could now see the roof of the cot-tage where Paul had lived with his wife and the abbé. "Suppose the abbé's there?" he asked.

Wat appeared to weigh the possibility. "I doubt it. I should say he's most likely in the village, deep in confab-ulation with that miser Philip and your master and the big smith. If he is at home, though, just tell the truth—but not in too much detail, you understand. I wouldn't mention our going for Gil, for example. It might make it appear that you had too many chances to slip away and didn't use them. On second thought"—Wat touched the side of his nose with one finger, striking a pose—"you can tell every-one that you *did* slip off, if you like. It will make it easier for you, and Gil and I will turn our backs now to quiet any qualms of conscience that might trouble you otherwise. I wouldn't tell the old woman her pillowmate's dead at first, though; it'll upset her, and you'll get nothing from her after."

Mark nodded, reflecting that he probably lacked the courage to break the news to Old Sue anyway. Wat solemnly, and Gil sullenly, turned away as he began walking the last hundred ells or so to the dead sexton's house.

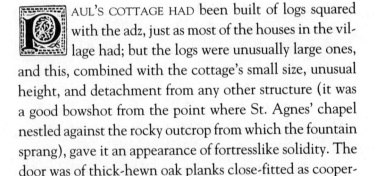AUL'S COTTAGE HAD been built of logs squared with the adz, just as most of the houses in the village had; but the logs were unusually large ones, and this, combined with the cottage's small size, unusual height, and detachment from any other structure (it was a good bowshot from the point where St. Agnes' chapel nestled against the rocky outcrop from which the fountain sprang), gave it an appearance of fortresslike solidity. The door was of thick-hewn oak planks close-fitted as cooperage and studded with a multitude of square nails. A brass knocker cast in the shape of a lumpy angel stood ready to strike an ecclesiastic note. Mark squared his shoulders and pounded resolutely.

Old Sue, Paul's wife, answered the door. She had been crying, making her eyes and the tip of her nose red. "It's you, Mark—by Holy Faith I'm glad to see you! Come in, won't you, boy, and have some buttermilk. You look worse starved than ever."

She pulled him in as she spoke, embarrassing him with

mothering—perhaps mostly because she was not always so happy to find him at her door.

"You're dirty as a scarecrow, Mark. Come into the kitchen with us and let me wash your face. You know, when you were missing too this morning, and Josie, I thought, 'Holy Saints, perhaps they're with the good man'—but then Josie came back and said Wat had you, but she'd not seen my Paul." The red-faced old woman stopped abruptly and took Mark by the shoulders to make him look at her. "Have you seen my Paul? You tell me truly, Mark Motherless; do you know what's happened to Paul?"

Mark wrenched himself away with an effort. "I don't know what befell him, Sue, truthfully I don't."

It was true, as he told himself when he said it, though it did not make him feel much better. But it made her let him go, and as they went down the dark little hall to the kitchen, the old woman seemed almost to have forgotten him already.

A cracked voice called through the kitchen door, "Who's come, Susan?" and Mark, though he recognized it, could not for a moment credit his ears.

As she sat on a chest close by Old Sue's kitchen table, Mother Cloot seemed far removed from the weak and mewing old wretch he and Wat had left that morning. Her shawl, perhaps for the first time in weeks, was off her head; sparse and dirty white hair framed her face like fungus around a stump. But there was vigor in every movement, and her bright eyes danced from Mark to the sexton's wife and back in a way both energetic and malicious. Mark noticed with a start that her pupils were almost invisible, like those of the charcoal burners' virgin.

"Mark dear," she said, "you're a pleasure to see again,

that helped me down so kindly this morning. And where'd you get your hatchet?

"Do you know," she continued to Sue without giving Mark time to answer, "this brave boy slept in my humble cote last night? I'd no bed to lend him, but my roof kept the rain off him, him and that fine, fat, fire-topped girl he brought. Oh, there was more wandering in the wood last night than you'd have dreamt, Sue—but he'd not that chopper then. . . .

"Let me see it, dear."

Mark, who had almost forgotten the hatchet Gil had given him, let it slip between his nervous fingers as he pulled the handle up through his belt. It clattered on the flagstone floor with what seemed a preternatural din before he could grasp it again and hand it to Mother Cloot.

She made a playful chopping motion at his face that stopped just half a hand's width away. "A fine slicer! Not Cope's work, though—too rough for that. Been cutting firewood for Wat?"

Mark nodded wordlessly, unable to think of anything to say.

"Wat was with me too, Susan dear. I know, I know"— she held up one hand to stop Old Sue from speaking—"a bad man. But if the men can't stop his robbing and murdering, how am I to? An old, sick woman, eh?" She gulped, overcome for an instant by self-pity, but brightened again at once. "Here, boy." She slid the hatchet across the table to Mark again. "Stick this back where you had it"—she swallowed with more than her usual difficulty—"an' Sue'll get you some buttermilk, and a bowl of clabber from her crock. I was about to cast runes for Sue. You'd like watching?"

"Cast runes?" Mark asked stupidly.

"We knew one another when we were just girls, she and I," the sexton's wife put in quickly. "And hearing Paul was gone, she came to comfort me, like a good Christian woman."

"I never comfort another way," Mother Cloot said slyly, "never having wed, myself. Though there's them that come and see me of a night," she added, half, as it seemed, to herself, "some might not call men." The expression in her eyes frightened Mark, who was still trying to accustom himself to the idea that Mother Cloot—who he had boyishly imagined had existed forever just as she was now—was in fact no older than the sometimes charitable wife of the sexton.

"She's a good, kind woman," Sue said defensively, "and if she'd rather live alone, that's her own affair. Let me get you something to eat and drink, Mark, and a wet clout to scour that face."

"Ah, there," Mother Cloot said as soon as Sue had gone, "there's a fine woman—that's that afeared. The abbé'd not like my castin' in his house, but he's in the village, good man, and he's got naught to tell her." From one of her sleeves the old woman took a bundle of brown sticks a hand's breadth in length and no thicker than twigs. After a moment Mark saw that they were actually small bones, dark with grease and much handling.

"They know all, the runes do," Mother Cloot said softly as she untied the wisp of rag with which the bones were bound. "We've but to learn to read 'em." With a practiced gesture she tossed them on the table before Mark, who jumped back a little.

"Sue wishes these to find her man, but while she

soothes her head with wifery, we'll see what they've to say of you." Mother Cloot swallowed and snuffled. "Now then, dear, a rune is a letter. Not these." She pointed to one of the bones. "They're but the marks that runes are built of. Can you read, Mark?"

Mark shook his head. "What kind of bones are those?"

"Thigh bones of men." Seeing his incredulity, she began to sway from side to side. "Tell a lie and be a lawyer—tell the truth and be a trull. Murdered by me and their mothers, Mark; and every one is a left thigh bone."

"You can see the future in them?"

"Oh, aye. More ways than you'd know. Now see here." Mother Cloot pointed again, this time indicating a pattern into which four of the bones had fallen. "There's the first rune of your name, Mark. That one"—she pointed to another group—"means Josellen's, and that with the sword across it is Paul's. He's met hard comfort from the look." She wheezed. "See, with the sword gone"—she lifted a bone from the pattern—"it looks like this. Runes are all of straight marks, for they were made first for scratchin' on stones and the like."

Old Sue came back into the kitchen carrying a bowl and a basswood dipper of buttermilk, and Mother Cloot gathered up the brown bones with a sweep of her hand.

"Stand up," the other woman commanded Mark, thumping the bowl and dipper down in front of him and taking a wet cloth from her arm.

Mark did as she ordered and suffered a face-washing done with the thoroughness possible only to women with something to forget. When it was over, he was permitted to refresh himself with the buttermilk and clabber.

"Where'd you leave young Wat?" Mother Cloot in-

quired. "Not," she added with a sort of simper toward the
sexton's wife, "that I care a thistle for that slit-gizzard,
though when a body lives alone, most any that brings a
friendly word and a bit of meat is welcome. There's few
that call regular, I'll tell you."

Old Sue looked guilty, and Mark wondered if she had
shown her girlhood acquaintance much courtesy before
Paul vanished.

"I left him not far from here," Mark answered. "He finally let me have a longer tether than he had before, and
I thought it best to go without a farewell. Though I don't
think Wat's such a bad fellow, really."

The sexton's wife turned on him sharply. "He's an evil
man with a smooth tongue, Mark, and you're well free of
him, believe me. He's done some wicked things you're too
young to remember, and others that *that one*"—she jerked
her head at Mother Cloot, seeming to have forgotten her
recent friendliness—"could tell of if she would. My Paul
would never hear his name without spitting, for all that the
sneaking burners and woods runners think him half a
prince."

"Ah, the good folk." Mother Cloot was rocking herself from side to side again, as she had in talking to Mark.
"Nothing's too bad for them—if it drag down the wicked.
Lyin' in my bed this morn, I heard young Wat say he was
going away—wanted to tell the abbé about it and have his
blessing—before this strong stripling came to carry me by
the fire, it was. Now you'll have been telling the good pastor to pour a drop in Wat's cup—have you?"

Seeing that by chance or by some second sight (and
he felt the latter was the truth) Mother Cloot had fallen
in with the errand Wat had given him, Mark said quickly,

"They wouldn't fall upon Wat when he's asked for a truce, would they, Sue?"

"They would if they'd take my counseling." The old woman shook her head. "The abbé won't hear of it, though. Your Wat's safe enough; I won't answer for the village."

"I'd better be going." Mark drained the last of his buttermilk and licked the spoon with which he had eaten Sue's clabber. "Gloin will be worried about me."

"What's he ever given you but a beating and an empty bowl?" Old Sue asked crossly. Thinking of the abbé's refusal to ambush Wat had apparently destroyed the last of her pretense of cheerful calm.

"Don't forget your hatchet," Mother Cloot reminded Mark—quite unnecessarily, since it was thrust through his belt.

He tried to mumble something polite, a thanks for the food, as he left, but a moment afterward could not recall what it was he had said. As he shut the door behind him, he could hear the muted rattle of the brown sticks Mother Cloot said were thigh bones, as they were cast on the table again.

No one was in sight. He walked back to the spot where he had left Wat and Gil, afraid that Wat was somehow testing him and would put an arrow in his back if he did not, but there was no one there. He did not dare call out.

To his left the path wound back to the corpse of the old sexton; to his right it led to the sexton's house again, and beyond that to chapel and village. He hesitated, wondering if the wisest course might not be to walk past Paul's body to the river and then follow the river path until he reached some country where he was not known (he supposed such a place to be very far away) and might lead a fairer life. If he encountered Wat, he could say that he had come that way looking for him.

He had no sooner thought of this than he became convinced that Wat was in fact some distance down the path waiting for him. He turned around quickly and ran up the path again in the direction he had come. He hadn't the time nor the desire to analyze his feelings, but he wanted Wat neither hung nor victorious; he wanted to be a hero, to be respected in the village, especially by Josellen, and to respect himself. Most especially he wanted to spy neither for Wat nor for Philip and the abbé, and he felt he had been tricked into the one already and might soon be trapped into the other.

By the time he was back at the cottage that had been Paul's, he was out of breath. He slowed his run to an almost stealthy walk and overheard the voices of the two old women drifting through a window.

"You see this—his, and lying so square across the stem of it—that's martyrdom."

"Like the cross?"

"Aye, though usually 'tis higher. This one makes a body think of Peter and his cross that was upside-down. Here where the three have their ends touching, and the fourth dropping down from one of the corners, that is meant, perhaps, for a little ax or the like. And here's another name sign, close to that ax handle. . . ."

"Whose?"

"I'll not say. The runes play their tricks sometimes— and he but a boy. Let's have another cast."

Mark did not wait to hear more. If Mother Cloot could read things that had not happened yet in the little bones, why should she think he had killed Paul? And why didn't she know he had cut Paul down so that his body no longer hung with outspread arms in an inverted cross? The questions whirled in his mind like dead leaves dancing in a storm. But if she could not read these things—it was a hope bright against the nightmare pattern—possibly she would not know if he did something more with Paul's body, and somehow prevented its ever being found.

The dead sexton lay just as Mark had left him, even to the maple leaf over his eyes. He had been a man of medium size, and before he had to do it, Mark would have thought himself unable to carry his body. Now he found he could. With no certain destination in mind he staggered down the path with the dead man across his shoulders, seeing no more permanent hiding places than clumps of brush and rotting logs.

He was drenched with sweat by the time the path reached the river at a point some distance downstream from the ruined town of Grindwalled. With a desperate effort he was able to cast Paul's body in. It floated and caught on a snag a few feet from where he stood. He waded in after it, unmindful of the wetting he was giving his boots and stocking knife, and pulled it free, then pushed it out as far into the current as he could go and yet keep his feet. Then he slipped the hatchet from his belt and let it sink in the water. Though he was chilled, he rested on the bank afterward before starting up the path once more. The sun would be setting soon.

There was no lamp glow in the windows of the sexton's house as he passed, and he was glad of that. Farther up the pilgrims' path the chapel of St. Agnes was dark except for the tiny ruby spark of the altar light. He went inside and tried to pray, but hopes and terrors came crowding out the paternosters, so that when he rose from his knees he was not certain he had completed even one. He had not been down the dark passage that led to St. Agnes' grotto and the miraculous spring in years—it was a thing pilgrims, not villagers, did—but he went now and splashed the clear, cold water on his face. The statue of the girl saint looked calm and happy in the glow of the vigil candle the abbé burned there when there were no pilgrims to pay for votive lights. Crutches and staffs, all old, festooned the walls with moving, interlinking shadows.

It was night by the time he reached the village. Josellen's father had put up the oiled skin panes, made of the intestines of hogs just as sausage casings were; they let the light of his fire and his tallow dip candles shine through in a way more attractive to potential customers than if it had merely showed at the chinks of the wooden shutters most people used. The yellow radiance of these taproom windows seemed vastly inviting to Mark, promising food and drink and, in the unidentifiable silhouettes that passed between the panes and the light, company. But he was terrified that as soon as he entered he would be accused of Paul's death. After hesitating at the door, he circled around to the dark and shuttered part of the inn next to the stableyard and called softly at the kitchen door for Josellen.

The door opened almost at once, and with eyes wide with surprise Josellen drew him inside. "Mark! Where've you been? The abbé and—and"—she made a helpless, all-embracing gesture—"*everyone* thinks you're murdered."

He said, "Let me sit, Josie, and give me a scrap of something hot if you've got it. I'm nearly frozen." He drew the three-legged stool kept in one corner of the kitchen close to the cookfire and seated himself on it.

The girl said, "You've got to go up there. Wat's in our tap with that one-eyed burner who was here last night, and the abbé says if you've come to harm the truce don't hold." She was pulling at his sleeve as she spoke, lifting him more by the force of her personality than the strength of her arm. "Philip wants to kill Wat anyhow—if he can get Cope on his side—and my father's nearly distracted for fear they'll all knife one another right here."

Somewhat reassured to hear that the men were not discussing Paul's death, Mark mounted the short, twisting stair that led from the kitchen to the taproom and entered the tap through the small door behind the bar.

7

HE ABBÉ WAS arguing with Wat when Mark came in, and Philip was addressing Cope and Gloin as though they were a multitude; so neither priest nor bandit nor cobbler noticed his entrance. Cope and Gloin did, both half rising and trying to thrust words through Philip's tirade. Josellen's father and Gil, sitting near the fire at the far end of the room, saw him as well, and an instant later everyone was crowding around him, all talking at once while Wat filled the room with his laughter. With his great black cloak swinging from his shoulders and the silver-and-ivory pommels of his sword and dagger catching the light, Wat looked very fine, but Mark wondered about the provision that no one was to come armed; apparently it had been forgotten in the excitement when the militia discovered that he was no longer with Wat.

Gloin was demanding, "What happened? Where did you go last night?" And the abbé, stroking his balding temples with relief, murmured, "I've prayed all day for you and Paul, that you might be safe somewhere. . . ."

But the wayfarer's voice cut through the babble with booming good humor. "Nearly cost me my skin! You're a weaver between trees, you are!" And to the abbé: "You thought I'd done him to death, didn't you? He gave me the slip though, just as I said, you see.

"Mark, where'd you go when you got away from Gil and me? Off through the wood for fear we'd lay hands on you again?"

Mark caught the clear hint that the fiction of his escape was to be maintained, and fell in with it. "Off in the wood," he said, nodding, "and then to your house, Abbé. Sue gave me something to eat, but you weren't home. Wat never treated me badly. He just made me stay with him; still, when I saw the chance to get away, I did."

"Now then," Wat began formally, "now that my good faith has been demonstrated, can we get to the meat of this meeting?"

The abbé said, "You told Josellen that you planned to leave the forest. With that as the subject I am willing to talk all night if need be."

"I do so plan. Gil has told me that yestereve you were all complaining that the lack of travelers is starving you. Did it never strike you that I am as dependent on the bounty of the road as any? But there's no use in *my* complaining and seeking someone to blame. I have to do something, and I intend to do it—much as I hate to leave the greenwood wherein I know every tree and have so many good friends."

He looked so serious that Mark felt certain he had his tongue at least half in his cheek, and the abbé was smiling in spite of himself at the idea of Wat's keeping a shop of robbery; but Gloin, Philip, and Cope seemed to be taking the wayfarer's remarks at face value.

"Much as I love this forest, I say, I'm leaving. But whatever you may think, it is not cheap and easy for a man such as I to shift to a new pasture and establish himself. I have no horse currently—I was forced to sell my last one—and I must have my legs around a good one when I leave the safety I have here.

"Also, I need coin for my traveling expenses and to persuade a few of the good people where I next stop to give me information of comings and goings. And more coin to buy me shelter when I need it. As things are now"—he fingered the purse hanging from his belt—"though I am not quite destitute, I haven't the tenth part of what I require."

"Are you hinting," the cobbler exploded furiously, "that we are to subscribe a fund for you as if you were a needy family or a broken footbridge?" Philip was known to have money put by, and he apparently felt that if this were the case he would be called upon to make the largest contribution. Mark had long suspected that the cobbler's religious skepticism was at least in part engendered by the abbé's charities.

"Not in the least. I am merely explaining my dilemma. I do have, though I hesitate to propose it, one suggestion as to how it might be resolved. May I speak without prejudice?"

Several members of the audience nodded. Mark helped himself to a piece of cheese from the bar.

"I mentioned a moment ago that I have need of information wherever I ply my trade. I have such sources hereabout of course, and they have informed me of a remarkable party due to arrive here tomorrow afternoon or evening. A wealthy merchant, so I am told, has sworn a pilgrimage to St. Agnes and is traveling with a considerable suite. There are six persons in all, and I am assured they order none but the best wherever they stop."

"That may be good news to innkeepers," Philip said angrily, "but what is it to the rest of us?"

"Simply this: The man has a full purse and a good mount. His wife, who with her maid and a page and two footmen travels with him, has rich jewels. If I might have the picking of them, I'd have all I require to leave; enough over, too, to give good shares to everyone who aided me."

Several persons tried to speak at once, but Wat silenced them with a commanding gesture. "Now hear me. You granted me the right to speak without prejudice. With only Gil, stout fellow though he may be, to aid me, I would hesitate to attempt them. The principal thing in this sort of business, you see, is to show force enough that there's no resistance; and I hear the merchant's a hotheaded old fellow and his footmen brawny. But with a little help it could be done; indeed, it would be nothing: 'Stand and Deliver— Thank You—Your Pardon and Fare You Well.' If you had done it a tenth as often as I, you'd think nothing of it. For myself, to make things simple, I'd ask but the one horse and half the gold coin. The rest, jewels and silver and brass and half the gold and anything else you might want, you could divide share and share among yourselves."

The abbé was apparently too angry to answer, and the rest too stunned. Wat added casually, "Those who help me will only have to stand in the background holding arms while I do the talking and collecting. There's nothing to it, as Gil will tell you. Everyone will wear masks, of course. And then on my honor I'll leave."

The abbé let out his breath with a snort. "Our captain wanted to capture or kill you when you came to this meeting," he said in a strangled voice, "and I dissuaded him. I see now that he was right and I was wrong."

Philip said, "Let him finish."

"I am—" Wat was interrupted by the clatter of feet on the short flight of steps leading to the front door of the inn. As everyone craned necks to see who the newcomers were, the door swung open on Old Sue and Mother Cloot. The village woman looked haggard, but Mother Cloot was as bright-eyed as a monkey.

"We are come," she shrilled with gusto, "to announce a murder, cry the murderer"—clearing her throat, she spat on the floor—"and claim revenge."

The sexton's widow added in a voice that was barely audible, "Paul's dead; we found his body in the river."

The abbé, who had risen when the women entered, put his arm about his housekeeper's shoulders and led her to a seat. She was not so much crying as sniffling. She wiped her wet nose on the hem of her apron, but seemed unable to frame a reply to the abbé's whispered questions.

Mother Cloot took up a position in the center of the room with her hands upon her hips, her expression lively with happy malice. "I'll tell you," she said. "You hark to me now, you good folk. This poor woman came to me this noon with a good-morrow, how-do-ye, and all the talk of the old times and people—how sorry that she'd not come more to see me in my dog-kennel in the wood, but now she'd baked me a pie in her fine, warm house. And had I seen her Paul?"

"If you've something to say, out with it," the abbé demanded crossly.

"She knows I've the sight, and can do things you can't, for all your sweet smokes and fine robes." She was addressing the abbé alone now, and angrily. "And she wanted me to use it, though she wouldn't say right out. I knew what she wanted, though; I went to your house and had a bite at your table and was making ready to cast the runes when who comes in but yonder young spider with a hatchet under his belt he said Wat gave him. It was good Sue this and good Sue that—just like her with me—until he'd fatted on her food; then chains wouldn't of held him, and out the door and away." She paused for breath.

"I cast then, and there was Paul's name and the sign of martyrs, and the sign for an ax and the name of Mark!"

A shiver ran through the company, and there was a general shifting of chairs.

"Your fakery means nothing to us," the abbé said calmly, "but a court might decide to burn you for it. Mind your tongue."

"I cast again; the runes said, 'Down the pilgrims' path, south.' Sue and I, we know what's fakery and what's not. We did as they bid."

The sexton's widow said weakly, "There was a rope hanging from a tree."

"Aye, but nothing on it. I wanted to turn back then, but Sue went on and made me come too, said she'd never stop. And she was right! We found him, away down the river—followed the river path and found him in the roots of a drifted tree, face down in the water."

Nearly numb with fear already, Mark realized that the women must have been on the path while he was actually carrying Paul's body, and passed him while he lay resting on the bank.

"Where is he now?" someone asked. Mark did not look up, but thought it was Gil.

"We pulled him out and laid him on some rushes. You men'll have to come for him tomorrow."

The abbé said softly, "He is wherever his Master has sent him. His husk may be on the rushes."

"And hope the wolves haven't come for him first," Mother Cloot finished.

Wat said, "And how was he killed?" with an air of professional interest.

"A hatchet. In the back of the head when his back was turned." Mother Cloot gasped for breath and looked at Mark. "Ah, he's a fine child, isn't he? Look at him with his face to the floor and the cold sweat on him. The hangman won't turn his back on you, Mark; not if you've something in your hand."

"So you're saying Mark killed my sexton," the abbé said. "Aside from your foolish divination, what makes you think so?"

"The runes told me! And didn't he come right in there with his hatchet he'd never had before? When he walked on the Barrow Man's grave, I told him it was ill luck."

"Susan"—the abbé touched his housekeeper's shoulder gently—"when Mark came in and you gave him food, was there blood on his clothing or on the hatchet?"

The woman shook her head.

"Did he mention why he was carrying the hatchet?"

Sue would not look at Mark, but said faintly, "He told me he'd been chopping firewood for Wat."

"Now that the subject's come up"—the abbé looked

around at the company—"I believe something was said earlier, possibly by a slip of the tongue, about Mark's having gotten a hatchet from Wat."

In a slightly different tone he said distinctly, "Josellen, I know you're listening. Come out; I want to ask you a question."

The red-haired girl stepped hesitantly through the small door behind the bar, looking fearfully at her father.

"Josellen, when you came to see me this morning, you told me you and Mark went looking for Mother Cloot last night; and I have told that to these men here, to explain how Mark came to be Wat's hostage. Now, how late was it when you and Mark left?"

"Not late."

"Within an hour of the time we left this room?"

Josellen nodded, seeming to gain confidence. "I only waited until I could hear Father snoring."

Someone laughed.

"Did Mark have a hatchet when he went with you?"

The girl shook her head.

"Did Wat give him one when you and he met Wat at this woman's house?"

Josellen said, "No," and shook her head vigorously, making her red curls fly.

"Answer this very carefully, please. Did he have a hatchet when you talked to Wat in the morning and he gave you a message to bring to me?"

"No, Abbé." She looked around the room and added solemnly, "He really didn't."

"Thank you; you may go back to your kitchen."

Wat drawled, "You could have simply asked Gil or

myself when it was that Mark got his hatchet—it was 'bout the midday."

The abbé shrugged. "It's very good of you to tell us that, but I felt it might be better to hear from someone whom reasonable men might consider a credible witness.

"Now then, as many of you may remember, Paul was supposed to come to our gathering here in the tap last night. He did not come, and I believe—correct me if I err, Susan—did not so much as sleep in his own bed last night."

The widow said faintly, "I never saw him alive after he supped."

"And neither, I think, did anyone else excepting his murderer. Now what is plainer than that Paul died last night, probably before most of us had come to this inn? And how was poor Mark to kill him then with a hatchet he didn't get until nearly a full day later?"

Mark raised his face from his hands, looking from the abbé to Gloin and back. "I never killed a man in all my life." In spite of his efforts to control it, he found himself gulping convulsively. "I wanted to kill Wat while he was asleep, but couldn't do it."

"Now," the abbé finished, "are we going to let this vile crone and this bloody-handed highwayman convince us that an orphan boy, whom we have known nearly all his life, slew, in cold blood and for no reason, a man who had always befriended him?" He paused impressively. "When there is murder done hereabout, I know whose name leaps to my own mind, and it is not Mark's."

Philip began, "Well, there's the runes. . . ." Several of the others nodded. Mark's heart sank.

Wat walked over to where Mark sat and laid his left

hand lightly on the nape of his neck. Although the motion seemed friendly, the tips of Wat's fingers scarcely brushing his skin, Mark sensed that the touch could become a stranglehold in an instant. "No one wishes to hang the youngster out of hand," Wat said smoothly, "but I daresay some of us would oppose your letting him have the run of the world before a reasonable investigation has been made."

He scanned the room. "Mother Cloot, your art will aid us, I know. Gloin, you'd not want to sleep and work with someone who might have sent your friend to the grave, would you? You'll want this looked into?"

Gloin nodded slowly.

"Looked into by you?" The abbé laughed bitterly.

"I seem to be one, at least, that holds an open mind. I'd not find Mark innocent nor guilty on what's been heard so far. And after all, we can't very well call in the assize officers until I've gone, can we? Which brings us back to our first question. As I read your faces, I should say that Captain Philip and you, Gloin, and Cope stand in favor of my earlier suggestion? The pilgrim transaction?"

"Not I." Cope rose slowly and walked over to stand beside the abbé.

"The other two then?"

Philip nodded vigorously, Gloin more slowly.

"Five of us should do it then. They've only three who could be counted fighting men after all; the page is but a boy, as I hear it."

"Five?" the abbé said. It was obvious that the discrepancy in number had taken him off balance.

"Philip, Gloin, Gil, Mark, and myself. We'll be wanting to keep Mark with us, and he's obliged to support his master like an honest lad in any case."

"But we'll keep a close watch on him," Philip added threateningly, "while he has arms."

Unexpectedly Susan stood and walked halfway across the room to stand face to face with Wat. "I've been thinking about it," she said, "and I don't think Mark killed my husband. I was a fool ever to go to her"—she jerked her head at Mother Cloot—"for I know well enough from where her power comes, and who they were that found my Paul's lich for me so they could kill this poor boy with it. 'Twould have been better if Paul'd floated in the river 'til his bones sank. Let Mark go."

"I'm afraid it's a bit late for that," Wat said, waving her away. "I've plans for young Mark, and give notice that he'll suffer for it if they're interfered with.

"Now, Cope, if you and the chaplain there don't want a share of what's to be had, I suggest you and he escort this poor woman to her bed. Paul's friends"—he looked approvingly at Philip and Gloin—"will see to it that he's avenged if that's necessary."

"We're not leaving without Mark," the abbé said firmly.

"I'm afraid that's impossible."

As lightly as if it were a wicker basket, Cope picked up one of the heavy chairs and took a step forward; but Wat's long sword hissed like a snake as it cleared the scabbard, then seemed to fill the room with its bright threat. Standing to one side of the wayfarer and slightly behind him, Philip, reaching beneath his smock, drew out the curved knife he used to cut leather.

The abbé laid a hand on Cope's arm. "I fear all those who violated the compact and brought weapons have ended on the same side, my friend."

Looking toward the fireplace, Mark saw that Gil had a knife too, which he held by the blade ready to throw.

"Still," said the abbé, seeming to weigh the odds, "we might do it. The rest are only curs fawning about Wat."

He turned to where Josellen's father stood behind the bar. "Innkeeper, will you help us? With Cope's strength, and your aid, and God's . . ."

Josellen's father produced a heavy cudgel from under the bar. "There will be no fighting here, I won't have it."

Wat said gaily, "Have no fear. There won't be. A bit of butchery, perhaps; but no fighting."

"You won't assist us then?" the abbé said, ignoring Wat.

"I won't. It'd be best if you and Master Cope, though I value his patronage"—he inclined his head in a serious little bow toward the blacksmith—"left now before there's trouble."

"You would have us leave this boy to the bandit?"

Josellen's father said adamantly, "Any differences you have with Master Wat, or with Master Gloin or Master Philip, you settle with them outside."

Cope's face had been changing color as the innkeeper spoke. Mark saw a deep red crawl up the big man's neck and suffuse his ears and cheeks until they took on the hue of raw meat. Something hard and cold formed in Mark's stomach as he watched, for he sensed in the way Wat flexed his knees and balanced the long, two-edged blade in his hand that if Cope were to turn half away from him to raise the chair at Josellen's father, Wat meant to thrust at his exposed side.

At the last moment Cope set the chair carefully back on the floor and patted it as though it were a horse he was telling to stand still. Then he looked inquiringly at the abbé, who motioned with his head toward the door and went out, leading Old Sue by the arm. Cope followed him.

"Well now," Wat said cheerfully, "that's over. Thank you much, Master Host, for your timely assistance. My friends and I could not have managed without you, I'm sure."

He winked at Gloin and Philip, but the innkeeper either did not see it or chose to ignore it. "There will be no fighting in my tap," he said in his usual noncommittal voice, "while I am behind my bar."

"We'll settle it outside, I'm sure. Meanwhile, though I'm not running with silver, would this unlock the door to a room? A bed for myself with no company and a pallet for Gil, who'll be taking it with him." Still holding his sword in his right hand, Wat fumbled in his purse with his left and tossed a broad gold piece on the bar.

"The finest room we have, for a week, and meals too—both yours and his," Josellen's father said with alacrity, "and happy to have your custom, sire."

"I hardly think I'll be staying a week." Wat winked at Gloin and Philip again. "But you may keep what remains when I settle my bill." Carefully, to avoid cutting the soft leather between the throat and tip of the scabbard, Wat sheathed his sword.

Mother Cloot said, "Now, young Wat. . . ." Some of the fire seemed to have left her, and she did not bother to stand before she spoke. "Am I to have Master Mark to examine?

If you'll bind his hands, I daresay I can manage him well enough."

Though he tried not to show it, Mark shrank at the thought of Mother Cloot's sorcery.

"Ah." Wat waggled his head. "Their hands do have to be tied, don't they? Feet too?" He did a little shuffling dance, then kicked one leg until his shoe was higher than his head. "I suppose you'd tie those after you'd gotten him home, though. After he'd had a crack on the ear from your stick. Not tonight. You go home and stretch yourself on your featherbed, Mother."

"Justice must be done," Philip said pompously.

"That's so." Wat smiled at Mark. "But I fear Mother Cloot's fondness for seeing others suffer might make her examination harder than justice, especially if we weren't around to watch; and we need Mark, don't we?

"You"—he turned back to Mother Cloot—"get yourself along now or I'll help you with my sword point the first half league on the way."

As the old woman left, Wat's face took on an expression that was almost paternalistic. "Time for bed, nearly," he said, rubbing his palms together. "Host, will you serve the tuckaway round? It's to my chit, of course.

"Gil, I think we really ought to tie young Mark's hands; we don't want him to give us the slip again, do we? Our host will lend us a bit of rope, I'm certain."

Josellen's father drew the ale behind the bar—four jacks, which he distributed swiftly and efficiently among the four men.

"No ale for you, Mark?" Wat asked in a tone of surprise.

"Gloin says I'm not old enough for it."

"Well now." Wat stroked his chin. "Innkeeper, haven't you something here the boy could quaff?"

Josellen's father said, "I've sweet cider, sire."

"A jack of sweet cider then. Gil, tie his hands before him so he can still drink." The charcoal burner was preparing to bind Mark's wrists even as his chief spoke, and to Mark's surprise did it gently and not too tightly.

"For sleeping arrangements," Wat continued, "I propose the following: I shall sleep here at the inn; Gloin, in his weavery; and Gil with him to keep safeguard on young Mark. Our innkeeper will lend you a pallet, Gil, so you'll not inconvenience your host. Philip will have his own bed, I suppose, unless"—he looked at the cobbler—"you'd like one of us to stay with you?"

"Oh, no." Philip waved the suggestion away. "I've no fear of the abbé, or Cope either, if that's what you mean; and my house is as stout as a castle."

"Good!" Wat clapped him heartily on the back. "We're all bedded down then. I've a head full of plans for the morrow, but that's the time for you to hear them.

"Innkeeper, you serve a breakfast?"

"For those that pay as you do, sire, my daughter will cook whenever they're minded to eat."

"I'll meet all of you here, then, for a breakfast. Everyone's fond of eggs fried in grease, I suppose, and what the boar sits on."

8

S SOON AS he had been allowed to make his usual bed on the webstery table, Mark, with his knife still in his stocking, had begun to consider how easy it would be, once Gil was asleep, to clamp the hilt between his knees while he cut the bonds on his wrists. But now there was a soft tapping at the door, and he sat up, disarranging the unsold woolens that were his blankets in cool weather. He heard Gil curse as he rose form his pallet, and Gloin, carrying a burning rush-dip, was coming out of the back room that served him for a bedroom.

The door creaked as Gil swung it open, and Wat's teeth flashed in the sputtering light. Wrapped as he was in his black cloak, Wat looked taller than ever, and he seemed to enjoy the astonishment he saw on all their faces. "Well met, well met," he said in a voice at once cheerful and conspiratorial. The door closed behind him. "What, Mark! Still got your hands laced? Here, hold 'em out." The point of his long dagger flicked across the rope Gil had borrowed from Josellen's father, and Mark had only to give a slight tug to part the last strand. "Have a knife in your sock anyway, don't you?" Wat grinned at the other two men. "Mean to say you didn't remember it, Gil? I noticed it this morning at the magpie's nest, and he used it this afternoon to cut the sexton down."

Gloin clapped one hand to his forehead.

"So you knew it, too, and forgot it," Wat said, chuckling. "The terror of the king's highway, that's what you'd be."

"I thought you wanted Mark kept a prisoner," Gloin said weakly.

"I did. I do. Until Mark learns which way the wind blows and who his friends are. But you can bet your Sunday shuttle it's not to turn him over to the hangman, much less to that crazed hag who has such original ideas about eyes. No, when the shouts are raised to heaven for the punishment of the unjust, you may take my word my voice won't be among them."

Wat seated himself on the edge of the worktable on which Mark had been lying. "It was you, wasn't it, Mark, who put the old man's body in the river? I don't care, really, but I like to keep informed of what goes on."

Suddenly Mark was frightened again. "I went back looking for you and Gil after I left the abbé's, sire; you weren't there, but when I came back to the house, I heard Mother Cloot talking to Sue. The runes showed my name."

"So you went back and tossed the evidence in the river like a sensible lad." Wat sounded approving. "The rub was that Gil and I were waiting for you between the chapel and the village—just in case you did decide to do a bolt. When you didn't come, we thought you had diddled us, and we went on to the inn. Of course we weren't figuring on the time it must have taken you to drag that old box merchant to the water."

"It was almost dark by the time I got back to the abbé's," Mark said apologetically.

Wat laid a hand on his shoulder. "Now let me tell you a few things, Mark. In the first place, I don't care whether you knocked that old grouser in the head or not; if you did, I like you all the better for it."

Mark started to speak, but the highwayman prevented him. "Even if he had been a friend of mine, which he certainly was not, whoever opened his skull for him did him a favor. At his age what had he to look forward to? A few more winters, each seeming colder than the last; a few plates of soup to gum down; half a year in bed listening to his wife tell her gossips she wished he'd be quicker about being quick no more. Aye, and waiting for Death's visit in the dark at night. As it was"—Wat snapped his fingers—"he saw a flash of light, like you've seen when you stood up too fast and cracked your head, and the ground hit him in the face."

"But if he had lived out his natural life," Mark began uncertainly, "mightn't he have been able . . ."

Wat waved the objection away. "You don't really believe that, do you? No one will in another fifty years. If you'd ever spent some time in the cities, in the capital as I have, you'd know better."

Gil said, "That abbé's gotten to him."

"Not as much as he'd like." Wat laughed—the same wild, uncanny mirth Mark had heard when they were threading the trees in the forest. "You saw how he was trying to get this boy to stand on the trap tonight, didn't you? You've a head on you, Gil, even if you haven't your letters."

Gloin said weakly, "I thought the abbé was trying to help Mark; I sort of sided with him on that."

"He? Light us a fire in here, will you, old fellow, and I'll explain the meaning of the little show you saw tonight, since you don't seem to have understood it. Nobody on our side wanted to see your 'prentice at the end of a rope except your own Captain Cobbler. We'll settle his account later." In an offhand way the highwayman added to Mark, "The crone would have done you in if she'd had her way, of course; no malice, she just likes to play games."

Mark wrapped the soft woolens around himself and shivered. He was in that state of fatigue in which objects seem unnaturally sharp—as though swimming in a clear syrup—and ideas invincibly evasive.

"Your palms-singer wanted *me* killed most of all," Wat continued. "If he could have gotten somebody besides Cope fired up about it, he might have done it, too. Not that he really believes I killed his sexton; you're probably down in the parish chronicle for that already. But anything that gets me hung and buried safe under a crossroads will fill his purse."

"But the abbé himself proved I couldn't have done it," Mark objected.

"He found two people willing to testify that you didn't have the hatchet at the time Paul was killed," Wat corrected him drily, "so that he could take you without resistance, and, so he thought at first, with only token objections from me. The witnesses were your girl and the best-known cutpurse for miles 'round the Mountain. Don't think he was surprised at what either of us said, or that it changed his opinion. Who was it who left the village the very night Paul was killed and went into the wood to sleep in the witch's kennel? Who was it that went to visit Paul's wife to see if the body'd been found yet, once he finally got up enough nerve to come home? I had to claim you to save you from him, of course, but that's probably done you harm, too, in his eyes. I tried to pretend I thought you guilty to take as much of the curse off it as I could; if he saw through that, it must have made him gnash his teeth to see his own trick played in reverse. I daresay you think that if the soldiers were to come again, you could tell the abbé about me and go free yourself—but believe me, you're sadly mistaken."

"Do you think Cope believes I did it too?"

Gil laughed coarsely, and Wat said, "Cope believes what the abbé tells him; you ought to know that."

"I suppose I had better help you rob that pilgrim tomorrow," said Mark with a sigh. "Maybe with the money we get I can go away somewhere myself."

Gloin touched the end of his dip in the kindling he had laid in the fireplace. The wood struggled to burn, then flared up to light Wat's wolf grin.

"There isn't any pilgrim."

The weaver dropped his tallow-soaked reed into the fire and, squatting as he was, had to catch himself on his hands to keep from falling forward. Mark stared at the bandit openmouthed.

"No one that rich would come here on pilgrimage if his life depended on it; he'd be a laughingstock; that kind go to Rome or Loretto or the Holy Land. And if one of those merchants does have to come this close to the Mountain, he either disguises himself as something pretty near a beggar or hires half a dozen bullies to protect him. I ought to know."

Gloin looked stricken. "You mean there's to be no money?"

"Certainly there's to be money." Wat warmed his back at the blaze. "Plenty for all, and handsome. Philip's."

"Philip's?"

"Why not? Because he lets you call him your friend while he hugs his sack of gold? What are you to him, besides someone to hear him rant?"

"I couldn't." The weaver shook his head and stared into the fire.

"Whose house is next to your own here?"

"Philip's."

"And he sees you every day, hungry most of the time. Ragged. Stand up and look down at yourself in the firelight. I can see your ribs through the rents in your shirt. You know Philip has money, don't you?"

Gloin nodded. "He talks about it sometimes. Anyway, everyone knows it; he does a good business with the shepherds and so on and doesn't spend. He's bound to."

"And does he or his wife ever come around and offer you a bit of his bread? When was the last time he stood you a jack?"

"Last year, on his birthday." Gloin would not look at the wayfarer's face, but stared down at the floor, then at his own hands. "I could have done as well as Philip," he said at length, "if it hadn't been for the ale, and the bad luck."

"I wish you had." Wat's tone was suddenly warm. "You'd not have been such a sour clench-penny."

"I could never face Philip afterward."

Wat looked from Gloin to Mark and back. "He wouldn't know, you understand. And you wouldn't have to take it yourself, except from me. Now here's what you and Mark will have to do. . . ."

They gathered around him.

9

ARK GRABBED CONVULSIVELY for something that was always grasped too late, his arms and legs thrashing out with a suddenness that jarred his whole body.

There was nothing, no falling. He lay on the hard, familiar surface of the worktable with a springy layer of worsted under him and more over him, save where one foot thrust out into the cold. He could hear Gloin's familiar snoring in the other room, and Gil's breathing, an alien note in the accustomed house, coming from in front of the workroom fire Gloin had lit for Wat. He knew his own breath was making a white plume, a ghost over his face, but he could not see it. Bending his leg brought the cold foot against his warm thigh. He drew down his head until only his eyes and nose were above the cloth and closed his eyes again.

Outside, every limb in the forest moved forward and back once, and then was still again. He heard it. Far off—a long way for the ground to carry the message by its trembling—

someone was sitting up. The knowledge ran up the legs of the table and entered his back, so that his back knew and was cold and prickled with fine little hairs before the knowledge entered his mind. At first he thought it might be the hangman (to himself he called this personage Black Jack, the name the village people and the shepherds used most often) waking and feeling for his rope. He had gone to sleep thinking about that, and how it would feel if the noose were put around his neck and pulled tight up under his ear. The crowd would fall quiet then, and he would step or be pushed out onto the trapdoor.

It was not the hangman. The hangman was too far away for even the ground to know. The one who sat upright in his bed was staring straight ahead, out over the foot; not toward Mark but almost directly away. Mark knew that if ever *he* did look toward him, directly toward him, it would be unbearable. It would be worse than death, so that he would leap off a precipice or into a fire to be out of that stare. Very slowly the figure was leaning forward. Mark could feel the hands clamp one at a time on the footrail of that bed. The grip was like iron, but colder.

Gloin coughed weakly in his sleep. Mark had heard that cough before in the cottage where he had been born; the cool flagstone floor like the one in the abbé's kitchen; the black porridge pot on a hook over the fire; and his father's hairy, heavy dog, white about the muzzle, coughing and snuffling.

The ground recoiled, shocked. The worktable swooped beneath him as though it were a swing whose rope had broken. He turned over, grinding his belly against the table, holding the sides with his outstretched hands to kill the fear. The figure was standing now, and his feet held the ground flatly, directly on the damp, breathing earth. As trees do, *he* sought strength with grasping, rock-splitting notes. The first step shook the earth almost as the standing had.

After that Mark listened for each step. It was so long between them that he thought each time the next would never come. And each time he had almost fallen asleep when at last it came. Waking Gil and Gloin, running away, even staying awake himself, were worse than futile. He was a rabbit in a hedge, doomed if the marten saw him. He tried to pray, but the footsteps shook the words to gabble. The world rolled under him between the footsteps; he and the figure together shifted under the sky as the shock of each step came. In the back of his mind he knew this was not really so, that the world could not, did not, move beneath the stars; but it seemed so.

He knew, not knowing how he knew, when *he* reached the pilgrims' path. That was the first time he had become aware of *his* place; now the ground told him not only of a direction, but of a locality exact beyond belief. He knew the very spot in the dust that screamed beneath the step.

A web of chain mail, linked rings each flattened where the ends met and clinched with a tiny rivet, rattled about *his* knees. Mark felt the fine powdering of rust that fell from the rings. It was green. The rings had turned to greenness in their decay, as herbs did in health. Where the greenness had fallen away, the knees beating it out slowly like fine green snow, the metal was hot and bright and yellow. It began to chime when the green decay was gone; gongs struck by imperious lords in their tens of thousands, call-ing their servitors to battle with demanding yellow sound.

A sword moved back past the knees, then forward past the knees again, with alternate steps. The slow swinging yet produced a secret singing in the air, a sound that waxed and waned like a faint wind in a chimney.

The figure was passing the inn now. Moonlight must be shining upon him; the moon would be at the full tonight, and the figure, the sleeper who had waked at last, was clearer than before. Mark saw the horns rising from the helmet with the moon tossing between them. The steps were quicker now. The house trembled and rattled with each. *His* face, as he turned down the village street in front of the inn, was moving closer and closer to the invisible line that stretched through the wall to Mark. He was aware of the darkness beneath the helmet's brim, and the glow of the eyes.

He forced his own eyes open, knowing that what he had seen was still outside, feeling the shock of each step, though what he saw now was only the blackness of the dark woolens in the dark room. He threw them from him and stood up, the cold finding him immediately, everywhere.

It was quiet outside; the floor was solid now, the house mo-tionless under his feet. Gil turned and moaned in his sleep.

To touch the latch was to touch a viper. Sluggish now with cold, it stirred slightly and dangerously beneath his fingers. He drew the door toward him. The hinges creaked; the corner grated and stuck at the spot where it always did. Bright moonlight, narrow as a knife blade at first, then club-wide, then flood-wide, came through the opening. He closed the door again to a slit, astonished at his own temerity. Peering through the slit, he could see nothing.

The village street was empty. The mud left by last night's rain looked stiff and silvered in the moonlight. The trees were still, without the touch of wind. He breathed deeply, drawing the cold air deep into his chest. Telling his back it had lied, he opened the door more widely—icy stillness.

In the direction of the inn something stirred. A leaf, one of the first to drop that autumn, rustled across the mud. Bits of rubbish, twigs and dead grass, pirouetted in the awful silence. A whirlwind, invisible and manhigh, was moving through the village. Mark dared not close his eyes. The dream seemed nearer than he could bear.

10

OW," W AT SAID, "we have to get inside."
Mark looked around nervously. It seemed absurd
that the two of them should stand in the village
street in broad daylight discussing how to burglarize Philip's house, yet they were as alone as they could have been
in the midst of the forest. Philip, Gil, and Gloin had been
sent nearly to Shinleaf Shingle, ostensibly to watch for
the fictitious party of pilgrims, though in actuality Gil and
Gloin were watching Philip. The rest of the village was
far down the pilgrims' path at the chapel, attending Paul
the Sexton's funeral mass. Even Philip's fat wife, for the
first time in Mark's memory, had received her husband's
permission to attend—at their breakfast meeting Wat had
been able to persuade the cobbler that this was the best
means of keeping her in ignorance of their plans.

"He usually climbs in by the scullery window in back
when the latchstring is in like this," Mark said, looking at
the door. "There's that piece of wood nailed onto the door-
post so you can't lift the bar with a knife."

Wat said in his gravest voice, "One of these days Art and Reason will prevent honest men's making a living." He was cutting a slender twig from the linden that grew between the webstery and the house that held Philip's shop and home. "However, I know a trick worth a gross of scullery windows. Look here."

The twig had been cut just below the point where another smaller twig forked out from it. By slicing this off, Wat had formed a little hook with which he could reach through the string hole in the door and coax out the string—actually a leather thong.

"Wise people," he remarked philosophically as he opened the door, "not only pull their strings in but tie them up. One day I'll show you what to do about that."

It was dark in the shop, Philip having left all the shutters up. The door to the living quarters beyond stood open, and through it Mark could see the cobbler's dressing fire still smoldering weakly in the grate. He had been in the shop often before, in the house seldom. It made him feel unsure of himself, and guilty, to be here now.

Wat rubbed his hands together. "I believe you said last night, you and Gloin, something about Captain Cobbler burying his money. Isn't that so?"

"I heard him say something like that once. Perhaps he was only trying to fool me."

"Then he was trying to fool Gloin too, in the same way on a different occasion. I doubt it. We should always trust our neighbors, Mark, except when they say they've no money." Wat stepped briskly over the odds and ends of leather that littered the shop floor, and entered the house. "Now as a practical treasure-seeker I can assure you that in spite of all the tales you may have heard, people seldom bury money outside their homes. That includes my own fraternity, who are always being accused of doing it. There is just too much chance of being seen in the act." He glanced about at the various doors opening off the little smoke-blacked kitchen. "You don't know which of these is the cellar, do you, Mark?"

"That's the back door," Mark said slowly, "and I think those two go to the bedroom and the pantry."

"Then it's this." Wat jerked the last door open. "Right the first time. Stairs even, where most poor folk are happy to have a ladder. You'd think he was a carpenter. Look about for a candle, won't you?"

As they descended the steps, Wat picked up the thread of his instructions: "Entirely too much chance. Not to mention the risk of being seen making a later deposit or withdrawal—or just making certain no one's gotten it yet. So buried money's nearly always in the cellar. The clay floors of the humble, like this, are rarely difficult. The flagstones of the gentry can cause a bit more trouble, though often something can be done by examining each stone for marks. Always look in corners first."

Bent almost double, Wat was doing just that as he spoke. "Where red clay like this has been dug," he added almost to himself, "the color is lighter. That comes from turning under the grime. Look for candle drippings too, where there's no reason for them."

"Have you found anything?" Mark asked. He was becoming increasingly nervous.

"Not yet." Having shifted a barrel of moldering rubbish that had obstructed one corner, Wat was examining the floor under it with particular care. Finally he ran his fingers over it and shook his head. "None of these looks right.

Mark, I want you to go upstairs and bring me a pail of water while I look along this wall."

Mark did as he was bidden, finding a bucket behind the churn in the kitchen and fairly running to the stream with it. Wat poured out the water a bit at a time onto various suspect portions of the floor, explaining as he worked. "When soil has been dug, you see, it's not as compacted as it was before, even though its surface has been tamped. It'll fall in when it gets wet, just like a new grave after a rain."

"I don't see any place falling in now," Mark ventured to say.

"Neither do I, more's the pity. I've had my eye on Master Philip for such a while now that it would be a shame to miss."

He straightened up finally, setting down the empty bucket and wiping his hands on his thighs. "No use spurring a dead horse. It's just not down here; we'll have to go back upstairs and cut open mattresses no matter what Philip told you and your master."

"I thought you told Gloin you'd leave everything just as it was so Philip wouldn't discover it for a while," Mark said hesitantly.

"Never let a promise interfere with practicality." Wat held his candle up for a last look around; then dropping his voice to a barely discernible whisper that startled Mark, he said, "Hasn't it struck you that this is a terribly short cellar?"

Mark looked at the walls blankly.

"The house is small, but even so, this can't possibly go to the front of it. Upstairs quick!"

After practically pushing Mark up the steps to the kitchen, Wat strode into Philip's shop and began kicking scraps of leather into the corners. After a few seconds of this he said, "Ah!" and pointed to a spot close beside the stool where Philip normally sat at his bench. Almost hidden by the dirt that had been trodden in around it, an iron ring was set into the wooden floor. "Pull that up!" Wat directed.

Mark was afraid the task would be beyond his strength, but the trapdoor rose easily enough with only a slight creaking of dry hinges, and a crude ladder invited them into the darkness below. Wat began to descend immediately, grasping his candle with one hand while using the other to swing himself down the ladder.

"Bring another bucket of water," he called. "This place is bare as a dancing floor; we'll do it in a hurry."

Since they had left the bucket in the other cellar, the fetching took some time. Mark had to bring it up before he could duck out the back door again to fill it at the little stream that was the village's water supply. As he was reentering Philip's shop with the three-quarters full pail, he heard a sound outside that made him set it down quietly and creep to a window to peer through a crack in the shutter. The noise had been a knocking, as of wood against wood, and as he looked, he heard it again—though he could see nothing through the narrow crevice between the boards. There was a rattling of metal, and the indistinct sound of voices.

Behind him, up through the trap, Wat called, "Never mind the water. I think I've got it." And a moment later: "Very safe he must have thought himself, sitting with the only entrance under his skinny posterior all day." Mark hardly heard him.

Before his eyes, suddenly because they were close to the

slit, a jumble of men passed. Then someone pounded on the door, no more than a foot or two from his head. A moment later he heard two blasphemous phrases spoken without emotion. The pounding began again, and another voice pronounced a lurid obscenity in an equally matter-of-fact tone; someone with a deep, growling voice said, "Come on," and there was a shuffling of feet. Mark waited, not daring to breathe. There was another pounding some distance away, apparently at the door of Gloin's webstery.

He turned and found Wat close behind him; the wayfarer held a small iron chest in one hand and his dagger in the other. "Men," Mark whispered. "Some of them in . . ." He groped helplessly for a word, tongue-tied with anxiety. "In iron tunics. Not stiff, little hoops. They had round helmets too, like pots."

Wat, whose face had been as tense almost as Mark's own, suddenly smiled merrily. "Men-at-arms knocking dents in the peasantry's doors with their spear butts. Perhaps the abbé got in touch with his bishop about Paul with less than the usual clerical deliberation. In any case we'd better be out the kitchen door and into the greenwood before they start firing thatch to produce a few citizens. I've the cobbler's mite right here anyway."

In spite of coffer, cloak, and sword, Wat ran the forest paths as agilely as a deer, leaving Mark hard put to keep up with him. When he stopped at last a good mile from the village, the boy was trailing well behind. "You need a few arrows about your ears," Wat told him, "to teach you speed. Does wonders."

"Are you going to tell Gloin and all of them?" Mark puffed.

"I suppose so. I owe it to Gil, and this will give Philip

something to think about besides my pilgrims. With a little luck I might even be able to make him believe that these Hectors you saw frightened them off. We'll have to do something about this temporarily, though." He looked disapprovingly at the cobbler's lockbox.

"You could bury it," Mark suggested.

"Hardly necessary. It needn't stay about here for long anyway; we'll pick it up on our way back. Walk down the path there a bit; then stop without turning around."

Mark slowly paced off fifty feet, then waited. He could hear Wat making scuffling noises behind him, and found himself thankful that the highwayman had not brought his bow, although he knew Wat could kill him whenever he chose. He would have to plan an escape carefully, for it was clear Wat would not let him go now, and equally clear that the longer he remained in the highwayman's company, the more compromised he became.

"Now off with us," Wat said close to his ear, "to tell the Travelers' Terrors they'd best get into church, even if it's only for the *Missa est.*"

The cold of the night before had turned the leaves. As Mark trotted along behind the black figure of the bandit, it was as though they traversed a forest on fire.

11

FTER A BRIEF exchange of news—about the soldiers' arrival and the pilgrims' absence—Gloin and Philip returned to the village while Mark and Gil followed Wat into the forest. They spent the night on the Mountain, bedded on the coarse grass that grew between the rocks, three and four feet long where it was not sheep-cropped. The impoverished mountain soil nourished only the rank grass, and on the grass, sheep. And on the sheep, a few people.

The next day, a little before noon, they visited a shepherd's cottage and found it deserted, though there was ample evidence that it had been occupied by a woman and at least one child until a few minutes before they reached it. A path threaded a maze of tumbled boulders nearby, and it seemed clear that they had been seen approaching and that the woman had preferred an indefinite separation from her dwelling to entertaining them. The remains of a fresh-killed sheep hung just outside the cottage, however, and they lunched on mutton and bread and water.

Working their way north around the Mountain, they came to the edge of the scarred sheep-grazing area in late afternoon. Trees, mostly fir and spruce, began to appear again, then with a disquieting suddenness became close-set in a needle-carpeted forest.

"If I had my bow," Wat said, "I'd take us a deer here or give you both leave to remind me of it after. I left it at the flea-ridden inn, though, and by now it's probably in the fire for fear the soldiers might see it. I'll be back, in time"—he looked at Mark as if he somehow blamed him for the loss—"and skin that fat innkeeper if it is."

"I could set out some snares," Gil suggested, "if you want to camp here."

They had come to a tiny rivulet that wandered down the slope of the Mountain, breaking with musical trills the enveloping and oppressive silence of the dark trees.

"We may as well." Wat seated himself on a fallen log to look the area over. "If we build a fire in that low spot, it ought to be sheltered enough, and no one could see it anyway with all this timber about."

To Mark he added, "Best of all, I've never camped here before; in my profession that's one of the best recommendations a campsite can have." It was a resumption of his old lecturing tone.

Mark ventured to say, "I hope Gil can get us something to eat."

"Oh, he will. Perhaps not much, but Gil can always find something, even if it's no more than a squirrel's hoard. I've some good caches myself higher up. If the pickings here are too thin, we'll climb a trifle more in a day or so and see whether or not they're still there."

Gil said, "It's safer to be by ourselves anyway." He

sounded relieved. "You never know when one of those shepherds will try to do you in for a reward, or sneak off behind your back to get somebody else to do it."

"Young Mark knows about that now." Wat grinned over at the boy. "Don't you, Mark? Remember when we went to pick up Gil?"

Mark nodded. Philip had insisted that Mark should be left behind in the custody of Gloin and himself, and there had been no doubting the cobbler's intention to turn him over to the soldiers, in the hope that having a prisoner would induce them to quit the village. It had shocked Mark, while making him feel enormously better about having helped Wat that morning. Still, he had been considering the events of the past two days during the long tramps across the sheep-lands and had come to certain conclusions as to where his best interests lay. Now he sensed an opportunity.

Gil had begun to gather fallen wood for a fire, and Mark moved to help him, sorting out in his imagination the arguments he meant to use with Wat.

"That leathersmith," Gil said at length, "is no friend of yours, lad." He had apparently been reviewing Philip's conduct as he worked.

"No, he isn't," Mark admitted.

Looking up at Wat, he added casually, "You're going to give me some of Philip's money to go away with, aren't you, Wat? You said you would."

"Of course, when it's time for you to go. With the soldiers about you'd be wiser to keep to cover, though. The roads are certain to be watched."

Mark took a deep breath. "I don't think they're looking for me. If the abbé'd sent for them, they'd have gone to his house right away, and they'd have been sure to have heard the people in the chapel. Then they wouldn't have been trying to find someone in the village."

Wat and Gil exchanged glances, but neither spoke.

Mark gathered more sticks, watching Wat as he talked.

"Three nights ago the abbé saw a fire up on the Mountain, and when you and I went to where Gil's people were cutting wood, you and he talked as though you were worried about someone farther up toward the summit."

Unexpectedly, Wat smiled. "You're getting to be a clever sprout. You're right; there's been a party of men-at-arms blundering around on my track for nearly a week. They came up the Mountain from the other side, thinking that because it's less peopled I had less chance of getting a warning, I suppose. I think I've told you I usually summer near the top; they must have known that, because they spent quite a bit of time poking about up there. Gil here had someone keeping an eye on them for me most of the time."

"Then it was their fire we saw."

Wat was grinning now. "It gets nippy that high up on these fall nights. Not that I should boast accommodations—I spent that same night up a tree like a squirrel, and so did you, as I remember."

Gil said, "There was but eight hardbacks and a forester."

"We can't be certain it's the same group." The highwayman sounded more serious now; Mark had learned that he was apt to mismatch his tones and meanings, but there seemed to be no hidden jest this time. "We didn't actually see them come down off the Mountain, you know; it's usually prudent to assume the worst—in this case, that there are two groups. That's why I implied the abbé might have sent for the ones you saw in the village. If they'd gone by the forest paths, they could have bypassed our fierce road-watchers easily enough."

"Wat." Mark had decided the time had come to implement the plans he had been forming. "Wat, let me go back to the village. I can find out for you whether there really are two gangs of soldiers, and when I leave, I'll get your bow and quiver from the inn and bring them to you."

Before Wat could reply, Gil snorted, "That bantam-cock of a cobbler will have you at a rope's end in no time."

"Him?" Mark did his best to give his voice a manly note of contempt. "If I hint to the soldiers that he was doing something interesting while the rest of the village was at mass yesterday, he'll kiss my hand."

"He probably would at that," Wat said, "but you're forgetting that he's probably accused you to them a hundred times over already. You might be able to get him into trouble, but it couldn't do you much good. Besides, the abbé thinks you killed Paul too. He'll draw a good deal more weight than Philip. What will you do if he's denounced you?"

"I'll think of something," Mark promised, "but I don't believe he will have reversed his stand so quickly, anyway. You're the one he'd like to see gone, Wat. I think I'll be safe enough as long as you're free."

Wat looked thoughtful, staring at the ground and pulling his chin, but Mark saw that he was watching him from under his brows as he meditated. "You'll want to leave in the morning, then?" Wat asked at last.

"I could go right now," Mark said, instantly aware that he had pressed too far. Wat was almost sure he wanted to betray him to the soldiers now. Mark tried to repair the blunder by adding, "It is awfully late; I suppose it would be nearly morning by the time I got home even if I walked all night."

Wat nodded, rising to stretch. "Nearly dark now. It's entirely too late."

Immersed in the delicate business of trying to light a fire with flint and steel, Gil had apparently lost interest in the conversation. Mark took a step toward him and made a pretense of trying to shield the sparks from the night breeze that had begun to stir. "Remember when you had me go into the abbé's house?" he asked Wat. "I did look for you and Gil when I came out; I really did."

"You were in there a Devil of a long time," Gil remarked without looking up. Mark heard his flint rasp on the striker and kept his eyes on Wat.

"Sleep here tonight," the highwayman suggested, "and you can leave in the morning. I'll tell you about a trail I know that will lead you straight there." Then his dagger leaped from its sheath and drove toward Mark's beltline in the fluid, swift motion of a swordsman's long thrust. Mark had been expecting it and jumped frantically back, over Gil's little stack of sticks and pine needles; just below his ribs the dagger blade came in, as though an icicle had been plunged into his flesh, bringing pain and the sensation of cold. He grabbed instinctively for the wound, holding both hands pressed against it as he dashed for the trees. Wat's boots were rattling the sticks of the unlit fire behind him. Something large whirred close by his ear just as he topped the lip of the bowl-shaped depression Wat had chosen as a camp. It was not until the sounds of pursuit had died away behind his careening flight that he realized the object had been Gil's ax.

Blood leaked from between his fingers, and his tunic and the right leg of his trousers were soaked with it. He knew he was leaving a blood trail that could easily be followed as long as the light lasted; in addition to the principal wound in his side, there was a second, smaller cut a hand's breadth behind it.

Times without number he slowed his frantic descent to a stumbling walk, then began to run again on hearing or fancying some noise behind him. Darkness came early to this, the north, side of the Mountain, veiling unexpected irregularities in the ground and hiding the roots of trees while he could yet see their trunks rising from the shadow. He fell often, rising with pine needles clinging to his sticky hands.

Worse, his entire right side was beginning to stiffen so that even though he ignored the pain he could not move normally, his right leg hobbling when he ran. The initial feeling of cold in his wound had passed off rapidly to be replaced by a burning smart, which was intensified tenfold by any unexpected movement. As time passed, loss of blood made him lightheaded. He seemed, sometimes, to be floating in the air above his own head, feeling only remotely the cramp in his side, or the blow to his cheek when it was lashed by a branch.

Somewhere an owl hooted. Mark halted for a moment, realizing that it was nearly full night, and listened. There was no sound but the sighing of the forest in the wind. After two or three minutes he began stumbling downhill again.

The slope, the trees, and the night seemed to continue endlessly. Once he blundered into a rill and, pressing his face into the water, drank more than he could remember having ever drunk before in his life.

How late it was when he saw the fire he never knew. Some time after the turn of the night, certainly. The moon, waning now after its fullness of the nights just past, had risen and set without penetrating the evergreen boughs. In the deeper darkness that followed, the fire glimmered like will-o'-the-wisp among the distant trees. He gave no thought to who might be there. He would have gone to it in any case, even had it been certain that Wat and Gil were the kindlers.

12

ARK WOKE WITH the sun in his face. It was the first time in a long while, since the morning of the day Cope had found the peddler's body in fact, that he had felt warm on awakening; for drowsy seconds he reveled in it before a slight motion sent pain flashing through his side. He winced, then opened his eyes to see the familiar pink-tinted face of Josellen bending over him. Framed by her swinging auburn curls, it seemed marvelous and unbelievable, like some sign of good fortune in the sky. From above the top of his head a voice asked, "Is he awake?" and Josellen said, "Yes," and smiled. Mark tried to turn his head enough to see the speaker.

The lean intelligent face of the abbé came into view. "Don't try to sit up," the abbé said. He laid a hand gently on Mark's chest, and Mark became aware that he was swaddled in several blankets, though he lay upon the ground.

He said, "All right, Abbé," and found his voice sounded odd and far-off to his own ears.

Josellen's head reappeared, this time beside the abbé's. "Sue's making herb tea for him, or trying to. Hot stones in the bucket."

The abbé shrugged as though to say "it won't do any harm and may make her feel better." Mark smiled, then rolled onto his left side and sat up.

Gloin and Philip were coming toward him, Gloin with an expression of mingled worry and relief. A small fire, the one he had seen the previous night, he decided, was burning a yard from his feet. Across it Old Sue and Philip's wife were fussing with utensils.

Gloin said, "Mark, lad, I'm glad to see you awake. I thought last night you'd die at the false dawn; we all did. Who cut you—Wat?"

"Yes, tell us," the abbé said. "We're all eager to know what happened to you, if you feel up to talking."

"There's not much to tell, really." Sitting up had made Mark dizzy, and he waited a moment to recover. "When the soldiers came, Wat and the charcoal burner left and went up the Mountain, taking me with them. I suppose Gloin and Philip have already told you about that." He paused, hoping someone else would speak and give him time to collect his thoughts. Not knowing what had transpired in the village after he had gone made him fearful of saying too much. "We stayed that night on the sheeplands. Then last night Wat tried to kill me, but I got away from him and ran off. What are all of you doing out here?"

"Hiding," Philip said somberly. "The abbé will tell you about it."

Mark wondered whether or not the cobbler had discovered the theft of his savings. When he had been debating with himself whether or not he should leave Wat,

he had planned to put himself in Philip's favor by showing him where Wat had secreted the coffer; he felt certain
he could locate the spot again, and Wat had not had
enough time to conceal it very securely. It now occurred
to him that his knowledge might be difficult to explain,
particularly if Philip had not brooded over his loss until he
was more concerned about getting his money back than
about revenge.

"Philip and your master came into the church while we
were saying the requiem for poor Paul," the abbé ex-
plained, "and told me the soldiers had come. We went on
with the burial in spite of the news, of course; Cope dug
the grave, and I'm glad to say we were able to put Paul away
decently before we were interrupted. Then four of them
came down the path from the village and made us all go
back with them."

"They'd broken into our inn," Josellen interrupted.
"Father was just white when he saw what they'd done to
the door."

"They'd broken into the Broom and Barrel," the abbé
confirmed, "and were making free with the ale and eata-
bles. As they told it, there was supposed to be a royal
forester in charge of them; but he wasn't there and never
came during the time we stayed. In his absence a gross fellow they called a sergeant was in command. I believe the
appellation is intended to indicate a sort of unknighted
lancer, but there was certainly nothing of the gentleman
about him."

"From the way they talked," Gloin said, "I'm just as
glad the forester wasn't there. I think they were all afraid
of him, as bad as they were."

"We were certainly sufficiently afraid of *them*," the

abbé continued. "Even Cope was, though he wouldn't admit it; and we had reason enough. I don't suppose there's a person here who hasn't a bruise or a loose tooth to show. Only God and the Devil know what would have happened to Josellen if the men-at-arms hadn't felt compelled to wait until their forester returned."

Turning to Josellen, he added, "Pardon me, Josie, if this is painful."

The girl shook her head, and Mark suddenly realized that for once she was neither smiling nor scolding. It was startling to see those plump, familiar features looking so unhappy. "I'll get some more wood," was all that she said.

Mark asked the abbé, "Was it that bad?"

Old Sue was thrusting a wooden bowl of hot liquid to his mouth, and he took a swallow to satisfy her. It was fragrant but bitter.

"She'll get over it," the abbé said. "You young people are resilient, and she's only learned the kind of thing she'd soon have to know for her own protection in any case."

"How did you get away?" Mark asked.

"Just went," Philip put in a little curtly. "They didn't think we'd leave our homes, but we did. They were trying to extort gold from us, and by last night it was so bad we had to get away."

Gloin interrupted him to say, "The abbé came around to each of us and told us he was going to leave, and to meet him by the chapel if we wanted to come. And not to bring more than we could carry. I suppose they would have killed him if they'd found out. Anyway, Cope couldn't leave with us, and Josellen's father wouldn't; he said he was going to stay and protect his property no matter what happened, but he wanted Josellen to go."

"Is he all right?" Mark wanted to know.

The weaver shrugged uneasily. "He was staying right there in his tap when we left. Waiting on them just as if they were paying customers. It did seem to hold them down a bit, having him there."

"They're after Wat, aren't they? Did they say if they'd been up on the Mountain?"

"That's right," the abbé said. "But now if you're through with that herb tea, I want you to lie down and let me look at that gash in your side. We had to dress it by firelight last night after we were all so exhausted from tramping through the forest we could hardly stand. I think I can do a better job now, and I want to see it by daylight."

Mark lay down again, and allowed Old Sue, with Gloin's fumbling help, to unwind his blankets. Apparently his trousers and tunic had been removed the night before, while a bandage he suspected of having been an extra shift of Josellen's was wrapped completely around his body to hold a pad of rags against his wound. The rags were red-brown now, stiff with blood.

"I wish they'd taught us more leechcraft in the seminary," the abbé said as he eased the pad loose. "If it weren't that I had to help out in the infirmary now and then, I'd be lost in this parish.

"This is going to hurt just a bit, but don't move. No, this business of having one brother specialize in physic and another in chirurgery and so on is fine for the White Monks—they've got enough men to have one specialize in going upstairs and another in coming down if they want—but I may have to serve a turn as midwife before I'm done." He was silent for a moment, and Mark could feel his fingers probing the wound.

"Mark, was this a knife or a sword? Knife, wasn't it?"

"Yes, his dagger."

"I thought so, although it was held with the edges up-right like a sword. Lucky for you it was. But it penetrated completely, you see; the point came out the far side and made this secondary cut. From the difference in width be-tween the two I suspected a dagger because a sword blade wouldn't have that much taper. It is a double-edged cut, of course."

Philip, who had been watching with Gloin from a lit-tle distance off, called, "Why'd you say it was fortunate for him it was held like a sword?" Mark wondered if Philip still fancied himself as a captain of soldiery after all that had happened.

"Because the muscles run vertically in that part of the body." The abbé was beginning to replace the dressing, but seemed to enjoy talking as he worked. "A knife fighter holds his blade horizontally when he makes a stab, to go between the ribs more easily; because he does, a stab in this area is likely to sever a number of fibers. A swordsman fights with his blade held up and down; that way he can make quartering cuts to his opponent's neck and shoulders. I suppose Wat has been trained by a regular master-at-arms at some time, so that he unconsciously holds his knife like a sword."

"It will get better, won't it, Abbé?" Gloin asked. Mark wondered at the concern in his voice.

"Of course." The abbé finished retying the bandage and dusted his hands together. "He's exsanguinated; that's the principal evil right now. Not that bleeding's always un-healthy, of course. It can be a positive benefit to persons of sluggish disposition, and especially to those liable to gluttony—drains off the gross and turbid effluences. However, it's certainly not indicated for someone with Mark's pale complexion and nervous constitution; and even if it were, a good chirurgeon would never take so much.

"Our concern now must be to hasten the natural restoration of what has been lost. The ancients, wiser perhaps than we, thought nothing superior for this purpose to barley soup; their gladiators had to have one cup a day at least. I believe modern physic inclines to the hearts and livers of stags; they are always found filled with blood when the animal is butchered, and of course the stag himself is a blooded beast in that he is a noble animal of the chase. Unfortunately"—he spread his hands and looked wryly down at Mark—"we have neither stags nor barley."

When they had left the village, Mark learned later, each household was supposed to have brought its own provender. As an unattached girl requiring chaperonage and protection, Josellen had naturally gravitated to the abbé and his housekeeper, bringing with her a ham and a huge loaf of bread from the inn's pantry. By the plan Gloin would constitute a party of one, but since he had had no food at home, he had brought none; and Philip and his wife, not with the best grace, had been forced to take him in.

When Josellen had told him about these arrangements, Mark had been afraid he would be expected to join Gloin on Philip's charity, but the abbé had taken the responsibility for feeding his patient as a matter of course. In truth, after the first day there was no longer much at either table. In the forest the antlered bulls bugled as if in mockery, for it was the mating season, the traditional hunting time, and the time when the quarry forgot its fear of man in the ecstasies of rage and lust that the abbé had often used as homey examples in his sermons. But none of the refugees had bows or any other weapon bigger than a sheath knife, nor would they have dared to use them if they had, for if it became known that one of them had killed a stag, it would free the soldiers from any remaining restraint of law.

Meanwhile, Josellen collected walnuts, and Gloin taught the abbé to set snares for rabbits—technically also a violation of the forest laws, but one that was generally overlooked. Since they possessed no kettle, Old Sue was forced to use her hot stones again to make soup of the bones from Josellen's ham.

Despite the lean diet the wound in Mark's side healed quickly. The abbé, when he was not at prayer or inspecting his numerous but largely unsuccessful traps, was incessantly warning him of the danger of reopening it; but on the second day after he had joined the villagers, Mark was walking about fairly freely. On the third he helped Josellen gather nuts for a time and set three snares of his own, feeling that he had a better eye for the presence or absence of game signs than the priest.

As a result of the trapping and gathering activity, into which Mark was able to enter only when its rewards were nearly past the free-coming stage, there had been a brief period when it almost seemed that they might support themselves indefinitely in the forest. But when the staples they had brought from the village were exhausted, it became apparent that nuts and herbs and an occasional hare could never be more than a supplement, and soon they became a meager supplement. By the fourth day the shortage of food and the increasing chill in even the noonday air had made it clear that they must soon either return to their village, scatter among the charcoal burners and shepherds as best they could, or leave the forest altogether.

At a general council it was decided that the abbé should return to the village to see if the soldiers were still there. It was felt, particularly by Philip, that his cloth would afford him protection.

That evening, when the abbé did not return, everyone spoke especially cheerfully and went to bed expecting the worst.

13

HILIP AND WAT, dressed in the helmets and mail shirts of soldiers, were pursuing Josellen, screaming, through the forest. Wat had his bow again and was striking her with it. She wore a cockade of green leaves, and Mark wondered where she had gotten them when all the leaves in the forest were flame or orange or brown or yellow. He tried to put his hands over his ears to shut out the cries, but then instead of Josellen being beaten he saw a fountain of sparks and heard someone cursing, though the screams continued.

He sat up and looked about, for a moment too numb with sleep to understand what he saw. Two men were scuffling in the ruins of the fire, the hot coals and smoldering stubs flying as they struggled. Josellen was no longer screaming because she had buried her teeth in the hand of a mail-shirted soldier. As Mark watched, she ducked under the man's arm and fled into the wood. The first faint light of dawn was in the sky, and it was bitterly cold as he threw off his blankets.

A determined-looking soldier was striding in his direction; the man swung his partisan in an awkward blow Mark somehow could not evade. The shaft struck the side of his neck just below the jaw, and he was knocked flat. Before he could get up, he was hit again, this time on the crown of his head. The blow dazed him without knocking him unconscious. All around him was a muddle of bare and booted feet and legs; someone wearing boots had a foot on the back of his neck, and something sharp jabbed at the small of his back.

After a time the confused sounds diminished, and a single harsh voice dominated the hubbub. The foot was removed. Hands grabbed the tunic Josellen had washed and mended for him, and jerked him erect when the harsh voice shouted, "Line up! Line 'em up!"

He found himself standing between Philip and Old Sue. Each was held by a soldier, just as he was; next to Philip he could see Philip's wife. A burly soldier said, "Is this all? What the Devil are you—men or mutton? I could have done better with seven curs."

The man holding Mark said, "Well, I got one."

The burly soldier turned on him savagely. One of the teeth in his lower jaw showed above the lip when his mouth was closed, so that with his thick neck and small eyes he resembled a wild boar. "Two old women and a boy," the Boar snarled. "And this bandy-legged beggar's ape." Mark could not resist looking sidewise at Philip as this was said, but the cobbler was clearly too terrified to resent anything.

At the Boar's order all of the captives had their hands bound behind them with strips torn from the blankets. The fabric cut into Mark's skin, and before they had walked a

mile toward the village, the prickling sensation of re-
stricted circulation had started in his hands.

He had possessed no real sense of the village's location
with respect to the camp. His knowledge of the forest had
been rudimentary before he accompanied Wat to the charcoal burners' kilns, covering only the area within an hour's
walk of the village and the routes of a few major trails on
which he and Gloin had journeyed to buy wool. When he
was fleeing down the Mountain after receiving his wound,
he had imagined the village enormously distant; when he
found himself plunged again among the faces he had
known most of his life, he had supposed himself to have
been in error and thought the village could be only a mile
or two farther.

   Now the march seemed to continue forever. The soldiers must have spent most of the night tramping out to
apprehend the villagers, and they were sore-footed and
bad-tempered. Neither Old Sue nor Philip's wife, the one
burdened with years and the other with flesh, could keep
up a man's pace for more than a dozen steps; and so the
Boar urged on the soldiers, and the soldiers cursed under
their breath and shouted at the captives, while from the
branches overhead bold red squirrels calumniated everyone. When Old Sue wept because her husband was not
there, Philip told her bitterly that Paul was lucky to have
died before this calamity struck, and that if she herself
believed in Heaven a tenth as much as she pretended, she
would wish herself dead too so that she could join him
there. Whereupon one of the foulest-mouthed of the soldiers kicked Philip.

*   *   *

When they reached the village at last, they were locked into one of the inn's cellars. Mark had little familiarity with the geography of the Broom and Barrel beyond the kitchen and the taproom; he was aware that a side door opening off the short stair leading from kitchen to tap gave access to a second and presumably longer flight down which Josellen's father occasionally went for wine, but that was the limit of his knowledge. Now he quickly became confused in the maze of crooked hallways webbing the extensive and (in his experience) always shuttered residential wing of the inn.

At last the soldiers drove them down a steep, dark stair and into a room whose door was fastened by a latch with a heavy drop bar. They were given no light, and as far as Mark could tell by groping his way along a wall, the cellar contained nothing except themselves and a pile of rotten lumber beyond which the cellar floor, damp everywhere, became a stagnant pool of icily forbidding water.

With Old Sue's help he managed to lay some of the wood on the floor to give them a platform above the chill clay. Then there was nothing more to do, and in the dark he found himself straining his eyes until they hurt, opening them wider and wider in an effort to see. It was hard to keep them closed, although closed they saw only the same impenetrable black.

Sue's voice said, "Mark, sit against me and we can warm our backs against one another," and he did so, finding her by touch and pressing his thin spine against hers.

"You've a bad bargain, Sue," he said. "You ought to sit like this with Philip's wife. She'd be as warm as a stove."

The fat woman, who had become so exhausted toward the latter part of the march that Mark had thought she was likely to die if she had to go farther, only groaned. Mark wondered vaguely what fear or urging had persuaded her to accompany Philip when he left the village. It was absurd to think of her with her roll of bedding and basket of provisions waddling through the forest after him, but she must have done it. He wondered if Josellen's pleasant plumpness would change in time until she resembled Philip's wife; he wanted to ask the woman how she had looked as a girl, but could not bring himself to speak.

After a long time Philip said weakly, "The abbé has made Hell real at last. If the church knew about it, he'd be canonized the minute he died."

"You think he told them where we were?" Mark had been thinking the same thing himself.

"Yes, indeed. The shepherd took his sheep to market and sold them. How much do you think he got? Thirty silver bits, that's the regular price."

Old Sue said sadly, "More likely he got his feet taken out of a fire, poor man."

Mark was a little shocked that she had not defended her employer more vigorously. Without reasoning about it, he felt it her place to deny categorically that the abbé could have had anything to do with their capture; his ideas of loyalty demanded it.

"Not on your life." Although Mark could not see the cobbler, he could imagine vividly his head shaking. "If he was put to the question"—plainly Philip was proud of the phrase, doubtless acquired on some junket to town—"where is he? Wouldn't they have put him in here with us?"

There was a slam overhead, then another, then another, regularly. They fell silent, holding their breath as sparrows roosting in ivy do when an owl hoots.

"Someone walking up there," Philip whispered, and after a moment Mark realized he was right. The slams had been only heavy, booted feet crashing on the floorboards above.

"What are we under?" he asked. He had been too tired to maintain his sense of direction while hustled down unfamiliar passages and stairs.

At his back Old Sue mumbled, "I think it's the parlor. I used to visit there sometimes with her—Josellen's mother—before she died. There was rush mats on the floor then, but I suppose they've been taken up." She sighed, and Mark could feel her back bend, as though she were resting her head on her knees.

"I didn't know the inn had a parlor," he said.

Philip sniffed in the darkness, implying that Mark was only an ignorant boy after all. "It's used for entertaining when there're very grand guests. Rich men." He paused to savor the phrase. "Noblemen. I suppose that if the merchant Wat thought was coming had come, he'd have had the parlor."

Mark smiled at the reminder that the cobbler still believed Wat's tale of the merchant pilgrim. To bait him, he said, "I don't believe the abbé told where we were; he wouldn't do such a thing."

"Little you know about it. Why do I waste my breath on a rattleheaded child anyway? Shut up your mouth if you don't have sense to put in at the other end, Mark."

"You think I killed Paul when I didn't," Mark said reasonably. "So why shouldn't you be wrong about the abbé too?"

"I told you to be quiet," Philip snapped. "Now you do it before I come over there and twist your neck for you."

Fatigued as he was, Mark was angry. Only after the first surge of it was past did he realize with astonishment that he was no longer frightened of Philip. Strangely, the realization did not at first make him want to insult or defy the sour little man. Instead he hugged it to himself for a minute in silence, reveling in a secret rebellion. Philip's wife grunted faintly, and for no definable reason Mark felt certain she had knelt to rub her husband's feet. He listened intently until he could hear the slight chafing sound. It infuriated him to think that Philip, who had wanted him hanged should be at ease now.

"If you're going to twist my neck, you'd best begin," he said, trying to drawl the words in imitation of Wat. "When I tell the soldiers what's buried under your bench, it will be too late."

The threat must have hit the cobbler like a blow. Mark heard his hissing intake of breath.

"You beggar brat . . ." There was a shuffling of feet on clay. Philip's crooked leather-knife was surely gone now—the soldiers would have taken it from him—but Mark could visualize his snarling face and outstretched clutching hands.

"You can't very well tell Gloin to thrash me with the yard-rule now, can you?" He could judge Philip's whereabouts fairly well from the sound of his feet and his breathing. When the cobbler seemed to be in range, Mark stood up quickly and swung the piece of lumber on which he had been sitting, making a long horizontal sweep.

He was too quick. The plank only whished through empty air; then the cobbler was grappling him about the waist, and there was a tearing pain in his wounded side. He brought one knee up sharply, and Philip let go, but

Mark doubted that his blow had done much damage. As though she had only now realized what was happening, Philip's wife began to scream. Mark lashed out with a kick that encountered nothing.

Something struck the wall about a foot to the right of his head—presumably Philip had found the wood. Crouching and opening his arms, Mark charged as the cobbler had. He struck his man hard and drove him back several steps until he tripped and both fell.

"What's that?" Philip asked. "What'd I fall over?" Mark was lying on top of him and had him by the throat, which made it difficult for him to speak. "Wha' was it?" Mark tried to pound his head against the floor, but the clay was too soft for him to inflict much damage that way.

"Mark, wha' was it?" Mark could barely hear him over the fat woman's shrieks. "Mark, le' me up, please."

The *please* held the satisfying note of surrender. With a last shake Mark released the cobbler's neck and rose warily.

Philip said, "Stop that noise," testily to his wife and cleared his throat.

"Sue?" he called. "Susan?"

There was no answer.

Mark said, "Sue?" and the cobbler murmured, "Feel around for her."

Bending down, Mark moved his hands in circles. The left touched something and he grasped it, then explored it with his fingers. It was an ankle. "I have her," he said softly.

Together they ran their hands over her in the dark. Her skin was warm, and her limbs supple and limp, but Mark could not feel her breath even when he put his face close to her mouth, or hear her heart when he laid his head on her bodice. Philip's wife had stopped screaming and begun to cry.

"She's dead," Mark said, and stood up.

"Do you think I killed her when I fell over her?"

Mark shrugged, then realizing the shrug could not be seen, said in a flat tone, "I don't know; I doubt it; she was old, and they drove her like a donkey."

The knowledge that she was dead was difficult to accept and was made doubly so by his inability to see the body, yet it drained all the anger from him. There was no blood, no open, staring eyes—or if there were, he could not see them. When he had found her husband's body, he had felt little besides the shock of death itself, the knowing that a person like himself now lay sightless, motionless, and unspeaking. For Paul, the man, the taciturn servant of chapel and churchyard, Mark had felt almost nothing save that his familiar face would be missing henceforth. But now Susan, Old Sue, was gone. A part of himself was gone as well, and he could feel the emptiness where it had been. She had been kind to him sometimes, more often shorttempered; yet a fraction of his existence had depended on her recognition of it. She would never scold him again for being dirty when he came to her kitchen, and that knowledge was an iron stake in his heart.

"Shut up!" Philip said. "Stop that blubbering. Can't you at least put your apron over your face like a decent woman?" It took Mark a moment to understand that the cobbler was speaking to his wife and not to him. The fat woman drew each breath in a deep shudder, then made a noise—*bub-bub-bub-BUB*—that seemed to shake the walls. Mark decided that she was trying to speak, but was unable to get the first word out.

Outside someone was pounding the door and shouting, "Quiet in there, or I'll kick you all blue!"

Mark and Philip yelled and beat the door on their side, but the soldier apparently considered his duty fulfilled by making his threat and went away. In time they grew hoarse and, by degrees, stopped their tumult; Philip's wife's crying trailed off into soft moans and gasps. At the cobbler's suggestion they laid out the dead woman, working together as best they could in the dark, crossing her hands over her chest and placing her feet together. After that Mark stayed away from that side of the room and sat beside Philip. Neither had any wish to continue their fight in the presence of death.

Several times they heard feet on the floor above them, and once there was a rush of trampling as though all the soldiers had run through the room overhead, but no one came to the door for them, and any words spoken were muffled to unintelligibility. Philip wanted to talk about priestly perfidity and the glories of skepticism, so Mark let him talk himself out, listening only occasionally when a novel phrase or argument attracted his attention. Once he went to sleep sitting up and only woke in time to prevent himself from falling over. By unspoken agreement a corner equally remote from Old Sue's body and themselves was designated as a latrine.

Mark speculated endlessly about what might have become of Josellen and Gloin, the only people in the camp to escape the soldiers' sudden descent. It seemed probable that the soldiers were still attempting to capture them.

Disappointment at not having taken Josellen was certainly one reason for the Boar's savage displeasure with his men after the raid. If he were the Boar, Mark decided, he would send a party of men around to the shepherds' and the burners' camps to terrorize them into handing over the people he sought. He wondered if the real Boar were doing that, and if Josellen had found any refuge at all. He was still speculating about it when he fell asleep.

Suddenly there was light, blinding and glaring, making him raise his hands to shield his eyes. A soldier holding a torch had thrown open the door and was coming into the room. Without saying a word, and before any of them had recovered from their surprise sufficiently to speak, he grabbed Philip by one arm and jerked him up. Mark thought of darting out the open door behind him, but it was already too late. Dragging the cobbler, the soldier had passed through the door and slammed it shut behind him. The sudden return of darkness was like a blow. Philip's wife began to cry again.

Mark had half risen; now he seated himself. There was nothing he could do, no place he could go. Groping clumsily at first, he patted the fat woman on the shoulder; but in her grief she did not seem to feel his hand or hear his voice when he spoke to her. He moved a few feet away and settled himself into himself again. Perhaps Philip would tell them about Old Sue's body, and more soldiers would come and carry it away. That at least would be something. He found he was eager to see them, to have the excitement of light again, and of men moving about. He located the door by touch and seated himself alongside it, determined this time to slip out if the opportunity were presented. He listened for the coming soldiers.

Footsteps sounded overhead instead. First one man walking heavily and slowly, almost like Cope. Then several in a confused clatter together. Then a thump and two men walking out together nearly in step. A dim murmur of voices. . . .

Mark wished heartily that Philip's wife would stop crying so that he could have at least a chance of overhearing what was going on above their heads, but it was no use. He could make out two voices—one of heavier and one of lighter timbre—but he could distinguish nothing of what was being said, even when it was, as the increase in volume testified, shouted. From time to time the slow, heavy feet paced the room. He had dozed off when the first shriek came.

He stood then, not knowing why he did. The sound of grunting told him the fat woman was rising as well, as enslaved by instinct as he, though unable to respond as quickly.

The scream came again, longer and ending this time in a bubbling gasping. Mark stretched his hands above his head and found that if he jumped he was able to touch the floorboards of the room above; but this, of course, accomplished nothing.

The screaming continued for some time—how long, Mark had no way of knowing. There would be periods, sometimes long ones, of silence or unintelligible talk; then the screams. Several times other persons entered the room, remained a few minutes, and left. As he listened, Mark became more and more convinced that it was Philip who was screaming, and he grew to dread the moment when the cobbler's wife would ask him if it were, or if he knew what was happening. She never did. As nearly as he could tell, she had never seated herself again, but remained standing, sobbing in the dark.

In time the noises overhead grew monotonous. It seemed to Mark that Philip would go on with his screams and silences and speakings indefinitely. He was still tired despite the catnaps he had had, and by now hungry, too, and despite the cold damp, thirsty. He had just decided to make an effort to sleep when the door opened.

14

HE FIRST THING Mark really saw was the parlor
door. The soldier holding him knocked his head
against it to quiet his struggles, and he saw the
old, brown, well-fitted planks as they flew forward to
strike him.

Before that he had been squinting against the torch
glare, and there had been a few moments when the soldier's hand was across his eyes, but that had been acci-
dental, a handy hold to grapple him with. Mark had not
planned to fight, only to slip away if he could; but from the
instant the soldier had grabbed him, he had punched,
kicked, wrestled, and bitten with a desperate fury he had
not realized himself capable of. There had been another
man-at-arms waiting at the foot of the steps leading to the
cellar door, so slipping past would have been impossible
in any case. Mark had been vaguely aware that this second soldier was assisting the first by holding the torches
and occasionally kicking his legs from under him, but the
one holding him had been the chief adversary in his blind

struggle. Only cracking his head on the door took the fight out of him.

The door swung open, and he was carried in, still dazed. He had never seen the room before. In times past Josellen's father had been a terror to him, so that while he was quite familiar with the inn stable, the taproom (where he had been welcome when in Gloin's company), and Josellen's kitchen, the rest of the inn had been as little known to him as the far side of the Mountain or the far side of the moon. The half glance he gave the room before turning his attention to the two men there told him that the furniture was better than any he had seen before, that the shutters were up in all the windows—as they always were in this part of the inn—and that it was night; this last from the absence of light at the shutters' chinks. The room was lit with wax candles as fine and thick as those the abbé used at Easter, and it was dominated by the burly figure of the Boar.

The formidable sergeant stood where the light was brightest. His fists were on his hips, and he looked at Mark in just the way Mark had often seen Cope look at a horse he was about to shoe—wondering a little how much trouble the animal would give, but confident of his ability to handle any amount. It was the first time Mark had seen the Boar without his helmet; his hair was black and grizzled, sparse at the temples, and thin. Except for his bare head he seemed dressed for a battle, in hauberk, hose, and great-boots. From his sword-belt trailed a blade as long as Wat's and three times as heavy, judging from the width of the scabbard.

When the Boar turned away from Mark, the boy's eyes followed his glance to Philip, tied in a high-backed chair at the other end of the room. The Boar drew a knife as he turned, a great long-edged fighting knife, so that for a second, as he stepped toward Philip, Mark thought that he intended to kill the cobbler. So did Philip; his mouth gaped, and his eyes, which had been half closed, opened so wide that it seemed the balls were free to roll from their sockets. But the Boar only cut the bonds that had bound the cobbler's arms and ankles, and then with a flip (so it seemed) of his left hand, tossed him into the arms of the soldier who had brought Mark. Philip made no resistance, and Mark, seeing the bruises about his face and ears, decided that he might be more than half stunned. As the cobbler was dragged out, Mark studied his retreating figure in an agony of foreboding.

"Now," the Boar said. His harsh voice sounded as though he were trying to make it friendly; he cleared his throat. "Now then, you'd be Mark, the weaver's apprentice?"

Mark nodded.

"You sit yourself down." To Mark's relief he motioned to a bench-topped oak chest rather than to the chair where Philip had been tied. "How do you fare, Mark?"

Experience had taught Mark to reach for some tangible benefit when adults seemed friendly. "I'm hungry, sire," he said. "I'm thirsty too."

The Boar waved the term of respect away with a deprecating gesture, and going to the door, shouted, "Innkeeper!" down the hallway outside.

Josellen's father came trotting in almost at once. His lower lip was swollen at one corner, and Mark thought he had seldom seen a man look less happy.

"We'll have some honest meat for this boy here," the Boar said, "and wheaten bread. Two bumpers of your best

wine too, and don't take it to the well before you bring
it in."

Josellen's father wanted to say something; Mark
watched him try to get up the courage for it, then failing,
swallow and hurry out.

"A scoundrelish, tricksy fellow," the Boar rumbled as
he shut the door. "Never trust innkeepers, Mark; like
strumpets, they've made a trade of friendship. The rule's
the same for both: Treat them rough and don't pay until
you're ready to leave.

"Now you look a likely lad, so let me tell you a few
things I've learned about you since I came here; then you
can tell me if all's true." Hitching his sword out of the way,
the Boar seated himself across from Mark and reached
over to tap the boy on the knee.

"You're apprenticed to a fellow named Gloin, who
seems from what I hear to be a bad character in a half-
hearted, half-witted way. When Wat the Wayfarer was in
this village, just before we came, some tried to blame you
for one of his murders, and when your friends hadn't the
force to rescue you, he took you for a hostage when he left.
If what that dirty-fingered leather picker I just threw out
told me was true, you escaped from Wat when he tried to
cut your gizzard out, and you stumbled onto the camp
these worthless villagers had made in the wood. Is that all
correct, boy?"

Mark nodded again.

"Then just so we're on a square, undoubting basis, slip
out of your tunic and show me the cut."

Mark untied his belt and raised the edge of his tunic
to show his wound, turning himself after the Boar had examined it to reveal the smaller exit wound as well.

"He had a pretty good try at you, didn't he?" the Boar said. "Another couple of fingers over and you wouldn't be talking to me now."

"That's what the abbé said too. He was the one who bandaged me. He said that a dagger like Wat's, with a double edge, almost always cuts something you can't do without."

"That's right enough," the Boar said judicially, "though in general I wouldn't trust anything that slippery bedesman said, and the chief reason for a double edge is that it lets you make a backhand cut. Did he tell you that?"

"No." Mark leaned forward, so interested in hearing something about weapons from a real professional soldier that for the moment he forgot his wariness.

"Take a look at this, now." The Boar drew his own knife and handed it to Mark hilt first. "See how it's made? The blade tapers all the way, and there's only one edge and a thick back."

Mark turned over the heavy weapon in his hands.

"That's a dirk. Your dumb civilians call everything except a spoon by that name, but a real dirk is one of the handiest knives you can carry. A fighting man has to worry about punching through ring-mail, and a stiff blade like that, small at the end, is the sort you need. Your high-horsed knight has a kind of hilted spike he calls a misericorde for the same job, but if he ever had to butcher a calf for the pot, he'd give it up. Even this forester that's supposed to be commanding us has a fancy two-edged dagger like the one that was used on you, but I don't suppose he's ever had to get the humbles out of a stag with it; he's the kind who has hunt servants to do his dirty work, Sieur Ganelon is."

"He's not here now?" Mark asked. He had never seen a royal forester and had been wondering about this one ever since Gil had mentioned him.

"No, he comes and goes when it suits him, and he's only been a half day with us since we got here—and a good job for you he isn't." The Boar looked aggrieved. "That *Sieur* on the front of his name means he's a master over other foresters, and he couldn't be any rounder, or any harder on poor folk, if he was a duke and those green clothes of his were miniver."

Mark nodded understandingly, wondering as he did what miniver was. A moment before he had been on the point of showing the little knife in his stocking to the Boar, but the talk about the forester had given him time to reflect that the soldier might not always be this friendly.

"The fact of the matter is," the Boar was saying, "that it would warm my heart to lay hands on this Wat while our Sieur Ganelon is off tending to his other affairs. It would take His Mightiness down"—he winked at Mark—"and show who's been doing the real work."

There was a rap at the door. When the Boar shouted permission, Josellen's father entered carrying a tray laden with smoking meat and two cups of wine. Mark fell on the meat with a will while the Boar was giving his attention to the wine. It was fresh venison, and Mark wondered whether the soldiers had been poaching for their own comfort, or if they had received—from the mysterious Sieur Ganelon—permission to supply themselves with rations in this way.

"You weren't straining the truth when you said you were hungry," the Boar remarked. "When was it you ate last?"

Mark had to think. "Last night before I went to sleep." It seemed so much longer than "last night" since they had rolled themselves in blankets in the camp.

"The guard didn't feed you while we were gone?"

Without being sure of what the Boar was talking about, Mark shook his head. Certainly the guard had fed them at no time.

"I'll have to let him know about that," the Boar said darkly. "He's a sorry, sulking grub-gobbler anyway; that's why I left him behind to watch prisoners. We thought we were onto that wily abbé of yours; he slipped through our fingers, though."

"Oh?" Mark was all attention. "We all—down there"—he gestured toward the floor with one gravy-smeared hand—"we thought you had him already."

"We did, for a while." The Boar had been scowling, but suddenly he chuckled. "We treated him a bit too gently in the way of sleeping accommodations, and when he saw his chance, he was off like a hare. Those fellows can make trouble for you with the church authorities, and with Sieur Ganelon gone and able to say it was none of his doing if there should be a stink later, I didn't want to be rough. Still, I should have had him watched more carefully, but we were getting ready to go out to round up the village run-aways, and things were a bit confused."

"Did he tell you where . . ." Mark almost said "we were," but changed it to "the village people were?"

"Him?" The Boar shook his head and chuckled again. "He had more stories than a frog in a cream jug, but when I'd heard them all through—"

"How did you know where the camp was, then?"

"His feet told me more than his tongue did, lad. One

of the pickets had got him as he came in and was able to tell me which way he had come; I was able to backtrack him as long as the light held, so we were well on the road before it got dark. I'd like to get that sly black fox of yours back now. Maybe when Sieur Ganelon gets here, we could teach him not to play his pranks. Would you have any notion of where he might decide to hide?"

Mark shook his head, but thinking of the abbé reminded him, tardily, of Old Sue's body still lying—as far as he knew—in the cellar. He began to tell the Boar about it and her death, but the soldier waved the information aside.

"The leather picker told me about it, and she'll be taken care of in time; there's no hurry for *them*. The leather picker told me a lot of other things, too." He looked significantly at Mark.

"You said he told you about my coming to the camp," Mark ventured.

The Boar nodded. "The trouble with that kind is that you have to rattle them around a trifle before you can be sure they're telling the truth. Not that I like to do it. But if you leave them nice and cool and collected, they think a lie is better. Now just to give you an example, I know that your little cobbler had agreed to help Wat in a robbery. You know that too, don't you?"

Mark nodded, feeling certain that any effort at concealment he might make would be futile.

"You see? Now I had that from a good source—Cope, the blacksmith here—and felt quite sure of my information, as the smith seems an honest fellow even if he's not much brighter than the horses he shoes; but do you think Master Philip would admit it?"

"I suppose not," Mark said, using the last of the bread to wipe up the remaining venison juices.

"Well"—the Boar chuckled—"well, yes, he would. After a time. But not at first."

"I hope you didn't hurt him badly." Mark found himself feeling sorry for the little cobbler; his anger toward Philip had faded with Philip's surrender to him a few hours before.

"Oh, no." Reaching out, the Boar rapped Mark lightly on the forehead. "That kind of fellow you never have to do too much to. It gets into his head, and what he thinks about it bothers him more than what you've done. I laid into him good and hard with that poker from the fire, and you should have heard him yell. It was 'Mercy in God's name' and 'For Jesus's sake,' like he was conjuring. It would have made you sick."

"Didn't he ask you to stop because he was your fellowman?" Mark asked. "That's the way he always talks."

The Boar looked contemptuous. "What good would that have done? Any time a little pig-bladder like that calls me his fellowman I'll have his teeth down his gullet in no time. He had more sense."

"I guess I don't know too much about it." Mark felt baffled.

"Ah, but you know some things. You knew about our little banty-cock when I asked you a few minutes ago, didn't you? Now I've got a few questions for you, and you'll save us a good deal of trouble by answering straight out. You'll admit I've been as good to you as a father? And remember, I'm not asking for myself; I'm here for the king."

Mark nodded to show that he understood. There would be no escape from this room. Stout shutters closed all the windows, and the Boar would have ample time to stop him before he could lift the bar that closed the heavy door.

"Now I asked you just a moment ago if you knew where our foxy priest might lay up, and you said you didn't; but I'd like you to think about that again. Any of his family live 'round here, for example?"

Mark shook his head. "He's not really from this part of the country, you know. Just sent here by the bishop. I think he's from one of the cities, sire."

"Well then"—the Boar smiled to show he held no malice—"well then, Mark, perhaps you can tell me someone who owes him a favor? Someone he's helped in the past, maybe?"

"He's helped a lot of people," Mark said vaguely. It had suddenly come to him that the Boar's poised expression and ingratiating manner might result from his having a number of names already in his possession. Mark doubted that Cope would knowingly inform on the abbé, but it would have been easy enough for the Boar or one of the other soldiers to get him to talk about the abbé's charities over a jack of ale, pretending to admire the priest's goodness.

"Surely you can remember who some of them are?" the Boar coaxed.

And Josellen's father would tell under pressure. Mark suspected it need not have been a great deal of pressure either. He named several forest families who were certain to be on one or the other's lists and among whatever information had been wrung from Philip.

"Ah!" The Boar leaned back in his seat and finished his wine, draining the very dregs with a smack of the lips. "That's better. Now about your old master, Master Gloin.

He's still wandering about in the wood, and Wat might get him. He's no friend of Wat's himself, is he?"

Mark reflected that if Philip had admitted his own involvement with Wat's scheme, he would certainly have told Gloin's, and that Cope had almost as much reason to dislike the weaver as he did to wish ill to Philip. "Wat wouldn't hurt him, I think," Mark said disingenuously. "He was going to help Wat and Philip and Gil with their robbery."

"Was he now?" The Boar smiled. "Well, if I had him to go with that Philip, I'd have two of Wat's people to show Sieur Ganelon when he comes back, anyway. And where do you think Master Gloin might hide himself, Mark?"

"They weren't really Wat's people, except for Gil," Mark ventured to say. "They never really robbed anyone, you know."

"The law will determine what's to be done, lad." The Boar endeavored to look virtuous. "My duty's only to see that they stand before the judge. In a minute I want you to tell me all you know about Wat and this here Gil too; right now I'd like to know about Master Gloin and this innkeeper's girl."

15

ARK HAD NO way of knowing how late it was when he was brought into the inn parlor, nor how much time he spent there; but it was certainly far into the night when the Boar finished with him and ordered him locked in a little garret room at the top of the inn. The shutters here were closed, but after the soldiers who had brought him had left, there was nothing to prevent Mark's opening them, and certainly no warmth to lose. Outside the stars shone bright as gems of ice, and a whistling wind was blowing.

The reeking tallow dip the soldier had left with him showed a pallet and some filthy, mildewed bedclothes spread upon the floor. Apparently the garret was intended to accommodate the servants of guests, but it had been long since anyone grand enough to travel with servants had stayed at the Broom and Barrel. Moving as carefully as he could, Mark laid himself upon the pallet and drew the clammy coverlet up to his chin. The Boar had not been as brutal with him as with Philip, but it was the first time

Mark, who had been beaten often with rods and switches, had felt the solid, clubbing power of a strong man's fists. The Boar had known his business too well to risk breaking his knuckles on the bony contours of Mark's face, and had stayed reasonably clear of the wound in his side; but within these limitations there had still remained an ample area, and when the Boar had felt satisfied that he had gained all the information Mark would freely give, he had exercised himself upon it to discover what further facts might be brought to light by force.

Lying on the pallet now, Mark knew with certainty that, granted the opportunity, he would kill the Boar. His pleasure in the reflection was considerably damped by the knowledge that it was most unlikely he would ever be afforded the chance.

Suddenly he was staring at the slanted rafters over his head, now wholly visible in new daylight. Outside someone was lifting, carefully, so it sounded, the large chest that the departing soldier had placed against his door as a reminder that he was not to wander. Without drawing his knife from its sheath in his stocking, Mark curled his right leg until the hilt was under his hand, and closed his eyes. The moldy chest scraped the floor a last time, and the door hinges creaked.

"Mark?" The voice was a cautious, glutinous whisper. "Mark? Mark?"

He moved his head slightly until he could see the doorway. The round, flabby face of Josellen's father was thrust between the door and the jamb. Apparently he had not seen Mark's movement; he called again, softly. "Mark?"

"You'd better come in and pull the chest back as much

as you can after you're through the door," Mark advised. "Nothing could look much worse than you standing out there with your head inside."

The innkeeper came in quickly, tried to manage the chest as Mark had recommended, then closed the door and stood hesitantly in front of it as if fearful of coming farther into the garret. "Are you hurt bad, Mark?" he asked. "I heard it—most of it."

"I'm all right," Mark said, sitting up carefully. He found it difficult to believe that a week or so earlier he had been in awe of this fat, frightened man. "You look as if you haven't fared too gently yourself," he added, noticing that there were fresh as well as half-faded bruises on the innkeeper's face. "You should know what it's like."

"I do at that!" Remembering how severely he had been beaten seemed to restore a bit of self-importance to Josellen's father. "I got it when Josie left, you know. Not just from *him*, but from all of them. They caught me in the kitchen—had me on the floor in no time. I've never kicked a dog, I swear to you, the way they kicked me that day. Down there, trying to cover my vitals with my legs and arms, you know, I thought I wasn't going to live through it. I really didn't."

"It must have been pretty bad," Mark sympathized.

"I was the only one related to those that left who was still here for them to take their spite out on," Josellen's father declared bitterly. "Old Sue went with the abbé; Gloin had no one except yourself, and you were already gone; Philip took his wife. And how they wanted Josie!"

"Are they asleep now?" Mark asked practically.

"Most of them." The fat man sighed, and the indignation seemed to flow out of him like the liquid that trickles from a rotting vegetable. "They always keep a couple in the wood outside the village to watch the main paths, but the rest are sleeping. Most of them were up all night; first it was trying to catch the abbé, then questioning Philip, then you. Of course they kept me up with them to fetch and serve."

"Maybe you'd better get some rest then," Mark advised, trying to bring the innkeeper to the point. "They surely won't sleep long after the sun's well up."

"Mark, if I tell them I must have someone to help me here, and they allow it, would you be willing to do it? I do need someone—the bunch of them are running me 'til I'm about to drop—and meanwhile everything's getting dirtier and dirtier. Would you?"

"If they'll let me."

"I think they will. They trust you, I think, at least as much as they do me. Cope had some good things to say about you when they questioned him, you know, and he's the kind they respect—all brawn. If they didn't trust you more than Philip, they'd have locked you back in the cellar with him and his wife."

"Did you listen when they questioned Cope?" Mark asked. "How is he?"

"All right as far as I know. He was in talking to them when the abbé and Philip and the rest left, you see; that was why he couldn't go with them. He was pretty unhappy about it, although he knew they were going and had told them not to wait for him; but it made him look awfully good to the soldiers. They think the others were afraid Cope would inform on them. Actually"—the innkeeper looked aggrieved—"I was the only one asked to go who could have and didn't; not that *they'd* show me any consideration because of that."

"Well," Mark said to comfort him, "you've certainly had the better of them so far."

"More than you know." Josellen's father bent down confidentially. "Mark, I don't think they'll question you again, at least not for a while, but if they do, can you keep a secret?"

"I won't tell them anything they don't know already," Mark said proudly. "I didn't last night."

"Josie and Gloin are right here in my inn."

"Where?" For a moment the idea seemed so incredible that Mark felt certain Josellen's father was lying; then he accepted it. There could be no reason for such a dangerous and purposeless fabrication.

"I won't tell you now." As though frightened already by his own temerity, the innkeeper took a step backward, bringing his back against the door. "Not until there's reason for you to know. There's no sense in your running all over before they've given you permission to leave this room. Josie's all right if they don't find her, but your master's hurt." Seeing the expression on Mark's face, he added quickly, "Josie's right there with him. She's doing all that can be done."

"What happened to him?"

"An arrow. It was just after they'd run away from the camp, according to her. She thought it was one of the soldiers; she heard him, whoever it was, prowling around the thicket where she and Gloin were hiding while she tried to bind up the wound—but I haven't heard any of them tell about it if it was."

"And they're here?" Mark was still having difficulty believing that they could be sheltering in the same building in which he himself was a captive—the soldiers' head-quarters.

"She couldn't just leave him under a tree, could she? She told me she thought of trying to get into Philip's or the webstery, but she knew there wouldn't be any food in either—anyway very little. Of course she could have stayed with Cope at the forge, but she wanted her father. They came in late last night, while that head soldier was talking to you."

"If I'm going to help you, will I get to see them?"

"Of course. Don't you see—that's just it. If there're two of us, there'll be one to watch and give the alarm when the other brings them food or whatever. You will help?"

Mark nodded. "Any way I can. How bad is Gloin?"

Josellen's father shook his head. "Pretty bad. He's terribly thirsty all the time. Not like he used to be," he added quickly. "For water." He paused, his head cocked to one side. "Did you hear someone out there, Mark?"

Mark had not, and said so.

"I'd better be going; I've been in here too long already. You stay right as you are. Remember, until I can get permission for you to help me, make them trust you as much as possible."

Mark nodded, and the innkeeper, opening the door as silently and slowly as he could, eased himself out into the hall again. After the door closed, Mark could hear the chest being moved back into place. He lay down and pulled the coverlet over himself again; there seemed to be nothing else to do.

16

ARK HAD EXPECTED Josellen's father to return for
him shortly, but hour followed hour and no one
came. His high garret was no warmer than a
duck-coop on a pole, and when he had slept for a time and
no longer wished to lie on the thin pallet that was the
room's only furniture, he wrapped himself in the coverlet
and seated himself on the window ledge to stare down at
the empty village street.

It looked so peaceful that it almost seemed to Mark
that Philip's wife might come waddling out of his shop at
any moment, bound for Old Sue's kitchen and a good gossip. Peering straight down at the inn steps he had climbed
so often, he spat, then watched his spittle shrink to a tiny
white blob three stories below. One of the soldiers crossed
the road and disappeared among the trees on the other
side; Mark spat again, then felt relieved when the soldier
did not return. It seemed strange to see no smoke rising
from the forge, no shepherds or charcoal burners coming
out of the forest to trade. He was just under the rooftree

beyond which the abbé had seen a scarlet point of fire high up the Mountain on the night he and Josellen had gone to Mother Cloot's; he could, and did, reach up and touch it with one hand.

As his fingers felt the rough, weathered wood, he heard a sound like the tapping of rain; in a few heartbeats it had become the rattle of drums, then the pounding of hooves. Mounted on a black stallion—the biggest horse Mark had ever seen—a rider in green thundered up to the inn door, threw down his reins, and leaped from the saddle.

He was tall, as well as Mark could judge from his high window, and wore a wide hat with a long feather in it. His spurred boot heels kicked the hem of a cloak the color of spring leaves, and a short hunting sword with a gilded hilt dangled from gold chains on his belt.

On the rare journeys to town Mark had made with Gloin, he had occasionally glimpsed wealthy men who wore silk tunics and robes trimmed with fur, but he had never seen anyone whose appearance approached the pride and grandeur that surrounded this green-clad stranger. This was Sieur Ganelon, of course, and Sieur Ganelon must be an even greater personage than he had supposed; Mark leaned over the sill to get a better view, and as he did so, the hurrying stranger looked up at him. He got only a glimpse of the face beneath the shady brim of the broad hat, but brief as the moment was, the stranger's eyes met his.

It took Mark less than half a minute to decide to risk the door. The chest, the token of his imprisonment, presented no obstacle. When he threw his weight against the door, the chest scraped along the splintering floor outside until the door had opened far enough to allow him to step out.

The night before he had seen the loft of the inn only in the feeble, sputtering light of the rush dip carried by the soldier who had brought him to the garret. Now it opened all about him; piles of broken and discarded furniture dimly lit by sunshine filtering through the warped shingles of the roof rose higher than his head to either side. The stairs would be as dangerous as the trap of a gibbet—he dodged into the maze of time-swept rubbish in the hope of finding some other way down, a less-used stair or even a hole in the floorboards through which he could drop to some room below.

There was nothing but dust and the ruin of years, no hole bigger than a rathole, no window—he found two—that did not open to a sheer drop.

The steps creaked under the weight of feet, and Mark froze. A moment later he heard the scuffle of boots and could follow the sound the men made as they walked toward the door of the garret to which he had been confined.

Someone said, "Right here he is, sire. I thought it'd be better to keep him away from the others." It was the Boar's gruff voice.

And a drawling one answered, "Oh, he's here, is he? Behind the wainscoting, I suppose."

Numbly Mark realized that he must choose at once either to reveal himself now, making some excuse for having left the room in which he had been confined, or to escape quickly down the stair, fleeing from the soldiers and the village as well, and taking the consequences if he were apprehended. If he ran, there could be no chance of seeing Josellen and Gloin, no chance of helping them. Feeling as if the ground had opened at his feet, Mark realized suddenly that if he fled they might be discovered in the search for him.

Yet to stay would be more dangerous by far; when he had glimpsed the stranger's face, he had only half—indeed, less than half—believed what he had seen; he knew better now.

He had made his decision before the Boar could collect himself enough to answer Sieur Ganelon's sarcasm. "I'm right here," he said, and stepped out into the cluttered hallway.

The Boar was standing in the still half-open door, looking into the garret; behind him Mark could see a taller figure resplendent in green silk and gilded cords and tassels. Both men turned at the sound of his voice.

"I should break your neck," the Boar growled. Clearly he was already furiously angry and searching for a target that could safely be attacked.

"There wasn't any place to go—" Mark began.

The sumptuously clad man behind him pushed the Boar contemptuously to one side to look at Mark. "A sturdy young beggar! So this is the ferocious prisoner I saw staring down at me like a gargoyle. You needn't have bothered to shut him up, you know, Sergeant; you could have found a hundred like him in the shadow of the castle."

"You said you wanted to see him, sire."

"So I did, and now that I've done it—twice, counting the time he looked about to drop on me—I can quite truthfully say I never want to do so again. Why are you staring at me like that, boy?"

Mark closed his mouth with an effort and managed to stammer, "You look so much like someone I used to know, sire."

"Thank heaven. For a moment I thought you lack-witted." Sieur Ganelon turned to the Boar. "You say this urchin could tell you nothing of the outlaw's whereabouts, Sergeant?"

"He says this Wat stabbed him—he'll show you the place if you want—but where they were camped when it happened he says he's got no idea. Over on the north side of the Mountain is what he thinks."

"I see."

Sieur Ganelon turned back to Mark. "I'd be fascinated to hear your opinion of my appearance when I've more time, but for the present I'll have to ask you to keep it to yourself."

"I will, sire," Mark declared quickly.

The Boar laughed to show that he appreciated his superior's jest, and Sieur Ganelon said, "Good. But now I must get these lazy churls to marching again or they won't catch anything but stripes from the lash. Meantime, if you must answer nature's call, begone with you; you may tell the sentry at the stableyard door I gave you pass."

Mark started down the stairs as quickly as he could, but realizing that neither of the men was paying any further attention to him, he halted halfway down the first flight to listen.

"Very well." The royal forester's voice came down the stairwell clearly. "You held that beggar-brat for me to see, and I have seen him. You wanted me to see the cobbler, and I've seen the mess you've made of him, as well as I could in that dark cellar. I *would* have liked to talk to the innkeeper here—those fellows know everything—but you've sealed up that spring. Don't bother to deny your handiwork there, by the way; I recognize your style. I assume you feared we might get some really worthwhile information, and that's a commodity you despise. Anything else?"

The Boar's snarl sounded like that of a kicked hound backing into a corner, though all he said was, "Not unless you wish to see the smith, sire."

"Since you tell me he's an ignorant man who's already imparted all he knows, his only interest for me would be as an example of what *you* would call ignorant. And while it would be entertaining to see a man who walks on all fours and roots for vermin with his nose, we haven't time."

"Say what you want, sire." The Boar's snarl was uglier now, a hound that would bite if it could. "Fancy talk and fancy words—but the cobbler's one of them; everybody says so. And he's coming with us no matter what you say."

Sieur Ganelon said easily, "He'll slow you down, Sergeant; and he's not worth wasting a noose on. Do you plan to carry him?"

"He'll come around when we throw a few buckets of water on him."

Their feet sounded on the planks, and Mark hurried downstairs, trying as he went to digest what he had just heard. Had Josellen's father been killed? Or forced to run away? It was even possible the Boar had cut out his tongue. He shuddered at the thought.

Outside the stableyard door he found a soldier leaning on his partisan, just as the forester had implied. Though he could not be certain, Mark had the vague feeling that it was the same man who had held the torches while he was being carried up from the cellar. He knuckled his forehead and bowed as low as he could, drawing one leg back in the way Gloin had once taught him.

"Your pardon, sire, but the Sieur Ganelon sent me to ask where the innkeeper is." It was the safest question Mark had been able to frame.

The soldier stiffened to attention at the mention of the forester's name. "You may tell him I fetched another fellow to help me and we laid him on his bed, just as the Sieur Ganelon directed, immediately when he ordered it." Then relaxing a little and leaning toward Mark, he added in a lower voice, "Tear into our sergeant good, did he?"

Mark nodded and took a step back. He had a fairly exact idea of where Josellen's father's bedroom was and wanted now to get free of the soldier as quickly as he could. "Did the sergeant do it?" he asked. "I didn't know."

"He says he didn't," the guard whispered confidentially. "Tried to tell Sieur Ganelon it was one of us. The man was lyin' right over there by the gate when I went to stable Sieur Ganelon's horse, you know, but there wasn't no picket kept here until now. I guess you knew him?"

Mark nodded again.

"Seemed a harmless enough rabbity kind of man. He's a good deal too free with whatever's lyin' to hand, if you ask me."

By the time he had pronounced the last word, Mark had regained the building and was flying down the maze of halls. He had to search several rooms before he found Josellen's father, but he had been correct about the general location.

At first it seemed that there was nothing amiss with the innkeeper. He lay upon his back on a sagging bed, his great, globular belly rising higher than Mark would have thought possible; he might have been asleep, for the thin wheezing of his breath seemed to fill the room, but his eyes were open. Then Mark saw the swollen purple welt along one temple.

"Are you all right?" he called softly. He was suddenly, chillingly reminded of the way the man on the bed had called to him that morning.

There was no reply. Mark tiptoed across the room and looked into the innkeeper's face, slack and sallow against the rumpled bedclothes. The eyes looked back at him, then half closed. "Are you all right?" Mark asked again. He laid his hand on Josellen's father's cheek; it was no more and no less warm than any other man's. The eyes opened again at his touch, then closed.

Outside there was a shouted order, muffled by the walls. The slow wheezing breath of the man on the bed made Mark feel stifled, though the room was cool. He stepped out into the hall again and back into the room he had searched just before finding Josellen's father. There he put his eye to a crack he had noticed in the shutter.

Sieur Ganelon's great black horse was already gone, and the soldiers were forming a ragged line in the village street. As Mark watched, Philip was led out with a noose of rope about his neck. He could see Philip's expression clearly, and he jerked his eye away from the crevice, irrationally fearful that he might himself be seen. Somewhere heavy footfalls clattered. He looked about the room for a place to hide should the walker come nearer, noticing consciously for the first time that the bed was rumpled as if someone had slept there.

For a moment he paused, listening to the footsteps pass through the tap and out the front door; then he examined the coarse linen bedclothes. Had this been the Boar's own room? The cloth was clammy, as though it had lain for several days, and he found a pine needle and two curling dark hairs on the pillow; otherwise the room was bare.

There was a sound of shuffling boots in the village street, and he looked out again. The soldiers were marching off—leaving. To make certain, he counted them on his fingers; they were all there, eight including the Boar. They stopped in front of the cobbler's house, all turning to face it, and the Boar went forward and dropped to his knees to do something with his hands. Wildly, Mark had the fleeting impression that he was praying; but when the sergeant stood again, a bright tongue of flame rose out of his hands, whipping in the wind. Philip must have said something, because one of the soldiers struck him, knocking him flat on the road.

Mark saw the Boar reach up and touch the flame he held to the thatch. It seemed at first that nothing would happen, but he held it there until slowly, then very fast, the fire sprang up. The Boar threw whatever he had been holding up onto the roof and rejoined his men.

Certain now that the soldiers were leaving, Mark ducked out of the room and ran down the hall to the tap. From the front door he could just see Philip and the last of them as they passed the forge. Behind him the inn was suddenly quiet with the menacing hush of a deserted building. The silence seemed doubly strange now that he was out of the unknown, alien section and back in one of the rooms he knew well. He wanted to run to the fire, but he made himself go to the bar for a piece of cheese instead, fearing the soldiers would see him and turn back.

Surprisingly a bit of rind was still there. It had a stinking, musty smell that made him suddenly hungry and aware that he had not eaten since the Boar had fed him the night before. Cramming the stuff into his mouth, he went to the doorway again. The soldiers had vanished from the village as completely as if they had never come, leaving the bright scarlet flames as the only sign of their passing. He trotted, then ran, down the road to the fire.

In front where the Boar had kindled it, the thatch was already gone. The rafters were bare black sticks in the heart of the blaze. Although it was clear that neither he nor fifty like him could extinguish the fire, Mark felt that he should at least make the attempt; he got a bucket from the webstery, filled it at the stream, and dashed the contents onto the blazing roof. The water hissed and was gone.

Between the two houses some dead leaves on a linden caught a few sparks and flamed up; but there were too few left on the bough for them to communicate the fire to one another, though several times Mark was forced to stamp out flames among the fallen leaves on the ground. Briefly and skeptically he tried to pray for rain, feeling certain it would not come; it did not. The crackling had become a roar; a great column of fire twisted and whipped in the breeze.

Someone said, "Hello, Mark, I'm glad to see you're safe," and he was as startled as if he had been struck. It was the abbé, hands on hips and wearing a very dirty habit, but otherwise looking much the same as he always had. "Doesn't look as though we can do much about it," the abbé commented conversationally.

Mark shook his head. "I tried to throw water on it"— he was glad now that he had—"but it's gotten too big. Were you hiding from them around here, Abbé?"

Still watching the flames, the priest nodded. "Down at

Cope's forge. I made a fine hash of trying to see if they'd gone, as I suppose you've heard by now. They had me before I ever saw them; I'm afraid I'd better stick to the pastorate in the future and leave woods-running to others."

"You got away from them, though." Mark could see that the casual words concealed a great deal more feeling than they implied.

"Too late to do any good. When I got back to our camp, there was just the fire—and the blankets; I saved some of those." For a few moments the abbé watched the blaze in silence. "It seems to be dying down a little now, don't you think?"

Mark nodded agreement. The thatch was all gone now, leaving the walls and floor to burn more slowly.

"Cope went down to the inn to see if anyone was left there. Run down and get him, and by the time you get back, we might be able to put the fire out and save something of the household goods."

Overhead the smoke writhed in a black column against the blue sky.

17

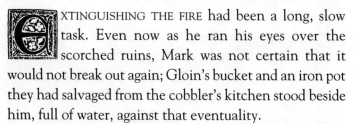XTINGUISHING THE FIRE had been a long, slow task. Even now as he ran his eyes over the scorched ruins, Mark was not certain that it would not break out again; Gloin's bucket and an iron pot they had salvaged from the cobbler's kitchen stood beside him, full of water, against that eventuality.

Half an hour ago the abbé had gone to the chapel. Cope, who had labored like a giant against the fire, had volunteered to attend to Josellen's father until the abbé returned, and to release Philip's wife and make a search for Josellen and Gloin as well. Meanwhile, the men had decided, Mark was to keep a watch on the fire. Mark had wanted to go looking for Josellen and Gloin instead, but the abbé had been firm.

It was not only possible, Mark thought, but probable, that Josellen was unaware that the soldiers had left. It was also possible that she was actually locked or blocked or nailed into her hiding place and could not release herself.

A little flame darted up from one of the tumbled

beams, and he threw half the contents of the pot on it, producing a puff of acrid smoke. The short autumn day was trailing out toward the edge of dark now, ending (to his still summer-rhythmed senses) too soon. The live coals that had been crushed to blackness by the sun's brilliance were now beginning to appear as ruddy smudges in the shadows. He poured the remainder of the pot over a particularly bad one, then looked around speculatively at the rest before beginning the short walk back to the stream to refill. Nothing else looked serious. A few of the cobbler's tools and a few more pots and pans might be salvaged yet from the burnt house, he decided, but nothing more. In several places the floor had burned completely through and fallen into the cellar.

It required only a moment to drop to one knee and fill the pot where Philip's wife had so often gotten water, where he had filled the pails for Wat. He raised his eyes from the smoothly flowing surface to see a dark, ragged figure standing no more than eight feet away on the far side of the stream.

"Good evening, Mark," Mother Cloot said civilly. "Would you help an old woman to cross this freshet?"

"There's a tree felled across it just behind Gloin's house"—he gestured toward the webstery—"and that's only as far as you could blow a feather from here. Use that." Her sudden appearance had unsettled him.

The old woman cleared her throat and let the resulting gobbet of mucus drop from her mouth into the stream. "And that's just what I had my mind on using. But an old thing such as me, Mark dear, can't balance herself like once. Wouldn't you come up with me—give me your hand?"

Mark did as he was asked, but sullenly, setting his pot on the bank in a secure position before walking up to the log that served as a bridge. It was nothing to sidle out upon it as he had done hundreds of times before and extend his hand to her, but he hated having to do it and sensed the old woman's own hostility. She had a surprising grip and vaulted up onto the log with more agility than he would have thought possible.

"Thankee, Mark," she said politely.

Without answering he turned and began to edge his way back toward the village side, his right hand extended behind him for her to grasp. He was just halfway across when he felt it wrenched. For a heartbeat it seemed he could not save himself; then he whipped the same arm forward in the direction of his fall, using the inertia of her body to heave his own body back into a position poised over the log. Briefly he felt Mother Cloot trying to do the same thing, but she had lost purchase by trying to release his hand a moment before; her convulsive grasp slipped from his fingers, and the splash she made as she struck the water wet his legs.

The stream was not deep, and he did not bother to look at her until he had reached the bank again. When he did so, she was wading out, holding up her filthy skirt. "I'm sorry about that," he said, helping her up the bank. "You'd better come over by the fire and dry out."

She nodded without speaking and hobbled to the smoldering ruin of Philip's home while Mark fetched his water pot. When he rejoined her, she was turning herself in front of the heat to dry her clothes.

"You've grown up, child," she said after a minute of silence. "This June you'd not have done that."

"I was trying to keep myself from falling." Mark felt ashamed of what had happened already, but not enough to admit it.

"Nothing wrong with that." Turning her back to the fire, the old woman drew up her skirt. "What befell the cobbler's house here? I saw the smoke, and that was what brought me."

"The soldiers fired it," Mark said. He felt uncomfortable under the old woman's sharp, malicious gaze and wished heartily that she would go away or that the abbé would return.

"I thought as much." She winked at him. "You didn't set them on it, did you, Mark?"

"Of course not."

"I came to see them, you know, before they caught you and the abbé and all the rest, and it was Cope this and Cope that until a body felt ill. They thought mighty highly of Cope, it seemed to me, and he was forever building you and the abbé up to them. He wanted them to hang *me*. Here he comes from the inn, not such a fine cock now that they're gone."

Cope was indeed coming, as Mark could see now that the dim figure in the twilight had been pointed out to him. "He's tired," he said. "He worked hard trying to put out the fire."

The old woman snorted. "I tried to tell them who Wat was and what he was and where he was, but would they listen to me? Not with him about—looking like a fat bull with his great, dull eyes." She twisted her head over her shoulder grotesquely to spit into the fire. "Talking of lunacy and witchcraft all the time. The abbé got free of the soldiers after they'd taken him, didn't he? I met some of them in the wood last night looking for him. Did they get him again?"

"Why did you try to tell them about Wat?" Mark asked. "I thought you were Wat's friend."

"Wat's a wolf that needs to be brought to heel," Mother Cloot said. "He'd like to forget who his old teachers were. But never mind about that." She stared sullenly at the road down which the Boar and his soldiers had gone. "Did they get the abbé?"

Mark shook his head. "He hid in Cope's house."

"He hid in my forge," the smith called sourly. He had come near enough now to overhear what they were saying. "In my forge; I had to have the soldiers in my house whenever they came." With one enormous hand the smith pushed back the forelock of brown falling over his eyes. Mark thought that he had never seen Cope looking so bitter and worn.

"And a blessing on you," Mother Cloot said. "The others—how are they? How is Susan; did they take her too?"

"She's dead," Cope said shortly. "Now be off and get yourself back to your kennel in the wood."

"Dead—really?" The old woman seemed pleased, and even poked Mark in the ribs with one of her bony fingers. "I'll have to find out about that."

"Not from me," Cope snapped. He picked up Mark's bucket and poured water on the glowing coals Mother Cloot was warming herself before. "Mark, Father's back at the inn, and he wants both of us to join him there. I don't judge this fire's still dangerous."

Mother Cloot followed them, as Mark had somehow known she would. Cope ignored her, allowing her to trail along silently twenty or thirty feet behind. Now that he had time to think, Mark recalled that Mother Cloot was supposed to be able to cast curses, and the memory of her easy forgiveness a few moments before bothered him. Several times he glanced quickly behind him to see if she were making mystic passes in the air or moving her lips, but if she were, she contrived to stop each time he turned his head.

In the inn tap the abbé had lit several candles and kindled a fire on the hearth, making the windows glow just as they had before the soldiers came. When Mark followed Cope inside, it seemed eerie not to find Josellen's father standing behind the bar calling down orders to her. Instead the abbé, looking troubled, sat alone in front of the fireplace. He seemed so distracted and deep in thought that Mark asked, "Is everything all right at the chapel, Abbé?" to announce that they had come.

"Oh, yes." The abbé looked up from his revery. "They rummaged about a little and took a few knickknacks, but I had managed to hide the communion service and the few other things of value."

Cope asked, "Can I carry him in to lie in front of the fire here? It must be cold where he is," apparently referring to Josellen's father. The abbé urged him to do so. He had no sooner gone than Mother Cloot came in, and Mark was startled to see that she had been crying.

The abbé stiffened at the sight of her, but when she pleaded to be allowed to see Old Sue's body, he seemed to feel he was not entitled to refuse. "Mark," he said slowly, "I'd better go with Mother Cloot myself. Cope showed me where Sue was when I got back from the chapel, and we'll return in a few minutes. Philip's wife is in the kitchen." He nodded in the direction of the stair behind the bar. "She wanted to be alone, which is understandable enough, but you might keep an eye on her to make certain she's all right."

Mark nodded agreement and made his way to the kitchen. Now that night had fallen, the inn was more quiet than he would have thought possible, and it seemed incredible that he could not hear Josellen and Gloin like mice in the walls if they were indeed there.

Philip's wife overflowed the little three-legged kitchen stool in a way Mark thought must surely be uncomfortable, but she gave no sign of noticing that or him. Her eyes and nose were scarlet from weeping, but she was weeping no longer, only staring at the floor across the monstrous paunch that filled her lap. Mark rummaged in the pantry and got himself several apples, as well as some bacon to toast on a fork in front of the fire. When he was back in the tap, the things he remembered most clearly about Philip's wife were the globes of fat that hung from her upper arms like mockeries of Cope's muscles, and her silence.

Cope himself had returned, and Josellen's father was lying wrapped in a blanket on the hearth. "You haven't found Josie and Gloin yet, have you?" Mark asked. He knew Cope had not, but it was something to say—something that might start the talk flowing again after the terrible stillness of Philip's wife.

When Cope only shook his head, Mark changed the subject. "Did you take Sue's body out of that cellar, Cope, or is it still down there where we laid it out?" He was hoping for an early return of the abbé and Mother Cloot.

"I carried her up and laid her on a table in the parlor,"

the smith said slowly. "That was when the abbé got back. I saw her when I went down after the woman, and when the abbé got back from seeing about the chapel, he told me to bring her up."

"It was awfully brave of you to hide the abbé," Mark said admiringly.

Mother Cloot's raucous voice broke in. "He's a fine man, strong and brave. The help of the afflicted, too— but let me have a look at that one now." She bustled over to Josellen's father and stared down at the paralyzed man's expressionless, contorted face.

"You gave him the viaticum, didn't you, Father?" Cope asked hoarsely while the old woman was examining the livid bruise on the innkeeper's temple.

"While you were fetching Mark."

"He's the only one that knows where Josie and Gloin are," Mark told Mother Cloot. He was beginning to feel that his master and the girl would never be found and was desperate enough to appeal to any possible source of help, however unlikely.

"Eh?" The old woman looked up sharply. "Tell me about it."

"Well, when the soldiers got Philip and his wife and Sue and me, they—Josie and Gloin—got away. Only somebody shot Gloin. He"—he gestured at the paralyzed man—"told me Gloin thought it was a soldier, but that none of them told about it afterward."

"Wat, most likely," Cope interrupted bitterly.

Mark shook his head. "Wat told me he left his bow here when the soldiers came. He didn't have it when I was with him." He took a deep breath. "Anyway, Josie brought Gloin here. Her father said it was while the soldier with the tooth sticking out of his mouth, the one I call the Boar, was talking to me; I guess that would be about right, because with Gloin hurt they'd travel a lot more slowly than we did. Her father said he hid them somewhere in the inn, but I don't know where and they won't come out. At least they haven't yet, and maybe they can't."

Mother Cloot said, "And you're hoping I can make him talk, sick though he is. It might be. Now, Mark, let's see if you can persuade your friends to do what's needful to help me—and only sense, too. Leave me alone with him. While I'm trying with him, you and the abbé and Cope can go all through this place—shout out Josellen's name. Even if she's locked in, she might hear you and be able to call through the door."

"If you think we're going to leave you alone with a helpless man," the abbé said coldly, "you're badly mistaken. Either Cope or I will stay here to keep an eye on you while you're with him."

"I'll stay," Cope volunteered.

"You don't trust me, Abbé? Well, you've no great reason to, I suppose." The old woman spat into the fire and stood with her back to them until the abbé motioned to Mark to follow him, indicated to Cope by a significant look that he was to watch Mother Cloot carefully, and led the way out of the room.

18

HE INN'S IRREGULAR plan—whole wings, cellars, lofts and galleries having been added piecemeal during the time St. Agnes' fountain was a popular shrine—precluded any really systematic search. The abbé had an eye for geometry, however, and contrived to miss little or nothing—though it seemed to Mark that they were forever climbing or descending stairs to confirm his judgments.

Mark showed him the room adjoining Josellen's father's from which he had watched the soldiers burning Philip's home; they examined it almost as thoroughly as they had the innkeeper's own, in the hope that if it had been Gloin who had rested for a time in the bed they might discover some hint of his present whereabouts.

"I don't really believe it was Gloin," Mark said at last. "You'd think there'd be at least a drop of blood on the linen, and this black hair doesn't really look like his. His is gray and brown."

Straightening up from the position he had assumed to

look under the bed (no easy task with a candle), the abbé snapped his fingers. "We've been thinking too much on Gloin, Mark. Don't you remember who stayed in the inn last—before the soldiers, anyway—and might have carried that pine needle you say you found? You mentioned it yourself in the tap."

"You mean Wat?" Mark reflected for a moment. "I suppose he would sleep next to Josellen's father if he could—to keep an eye on him."

"Or at least to make him think he was," the abbé added. "I believe you told me that Wat left his bow here and you tried to make that one of your excuses for returning to the village, but I haven't seen any sign of it; have you?"

Mark shook his head.

"Then I suppose that either Josellen got it—while she was still here—or her father did. In the latter case we may never find out what was done with it, but I'll wager it was Wat who slept in this room."

"Abbé," Mark said as they went out into the corridor again to resume their search, "did you see Sieur Ganelon, the forester, while he was here?"

"No." The abbé was looking speculatively at a section of the paneled wall. After a moment he rapped it sharply with his knuckles. "I was hiding in Cope's forge, as I told you. He was here for only half an hour, as I understand it. You saw him yourself, didn't you?"

"I meant before that," Mark persisted. "The Boar— that's what I call the sergeant—said something about his coming here and then leaving again; that would be while we were at the camp, I suppose."

"Cope might have seen him then."

The abbé opened another door, and they peered down a dark stair. "This is where they had you and Philip locked up, isn't it? I remember Cope taking me here to see poor Susan's body. I was carrying the host and went down before I gave Josie's father the viaticum, which I should not have done."

When the priest had shut the door again, Mark asked, "Abbé, what's the matter with him? He's alive, so his soul is still in his body, isn't it? And if it is, why can't he move and talk? It's as if he were tied with ropes we can't see."

"Now you're thinking that Mother Cloot has ensorcelled him, aren't you? And you'll be more afraid of her than you were before because of it. Believe me, his evil is no different from that of a dog with a broken back. His soul is neither injured nor enchained, but the reins by which it controlled his body are severed. It can still carry out its supportive function—which is why the body still lives; but its directive function is just as necessary. Unless he recovers soon, which I gravely doubt, he will die. He may quite possibly be dead by the time we get back to the taproom; you should prepare yourself for that."

"But his soul is really *him*, isn't it? And that will go on living?"

"His body has just as much right to call itself by his name as his soul does," the abbé corrected him abruptly, "and his body will die and rot like a dog's carcass until Our Lord calls it to live again. That is what we call *death*—the only meaning it has. His soul will exist forever, and I am glad you've learned that at any rate. I hope you also realize that the continued existence may be in Hell."

"I did see a dog with its back broken once," Mark said. "It was that stray talbot Cope fed for a while, and a horse

kicked it. It didn't act like Josellen's father, though. It
raved and snapped at everything in sight, but it did see you.
I saw it following Cope with its eyes when he went out to
kill it."

"And you wonder why Josellen's father doesn't look at
us or pay much attention when we speak." The abbé
sighed. "Mark, it's because the Talbot you saw was only a
dog, and this is a man. He is looking squarely at death now,
so nothing else seems important. The dog only knew itself
very sick and helpless. If I understand Mother Cloot, she's
trying right now to get him to tell her where Josellen and
Gloin are by blinking his eyes—or some such thing."

"You don't think he will?"

The abbé shook his head. "It's the kind of idea that
clever, cruel people think is certain to succeed because
they can't imagine themselves in the other's place. Right
now, if he is still alive, that man would give everything he
has or ever has had for a few moments of distraction, but
he can't have them. He may be able to tear his mind away
from the thought of death for a second, but no longer. No
elaborate codes and messages sent in signals. He's not like
a girl setting out the bridegroom supper at midnight and
looking for faces in the candle shadows. Not anymore."

"It must be terrible."

"It is his last chance to save his soul. Don't misunder-
stand me. A hero might be selfless enough to remember
his daughter's plight and single-minded enough to signal
her location by blinking. Or a saint might. Or, in all charity, a very stupid person like Philip's wife might do it—
someone who couldn't realize that he was going to die and
what death means. But not you nor I nor he."

"I don't suppose a physician from the town would come out here where there is no gold," Mark said dully.

"You're right, although I'll go and try to get one to-morrow, if Josellen's father is still alive. I'll feel better for having made the effort. But why should a physician come? Believe me, the best could do nothing for someone in his state. Only a miracle could save him."

They continued some way without speaking, opening doors and rapping on walls. Occasionally Mark shouted Josellen's name, then paused to listen. There was no sound save the sighing of the wind outside.

At last the abbé said, "Mark, I've been waiting for you to suggest one thing we might do for Josellen's father—so that I could feel I hadn't done such a bad job here after all. Can't you think of it?"

Mark paused in the act of tapping the ceiling. "We could take him to St. Agnes, to the spring," he said after a moment's thought. "Why don't we?"

"Thank you." The abbé inclined his head in a brief mock bow. "Not even Cope suggested it. I haven't done it because the man himself doesn't want it. As soon as I had finished giving him the last rites, I told him that when Cope returned I would have him carry him to the foun-tain. There was something in his eyes that made me stop when I was explaining to him the ceremony there—what prayers would be said and so on. I told him that if he did *not* wish to go he was to blink twice. He did so immedi-ately. But when I tried to find out why, or to question him about Gloin and Josellen or what had happened to him, I lost him at once. That's why I knew that Mother Cloot was unlikely to learn anything from him."

"Why do you think he wouldn't go?" Mark asked.

The abbé was quiet for a moment, collecting his thoughts. "I don't know, really. It's not as simple a thing as trying to find the people we're looking for or finding out who hit him. If I had to guess, I would say that he's afraid of a miracle. You're young, and you wouldn't understand yet what it would mean to a man his age to have his whole mode of thought swept from under him. He has lived here half his life, fattening on the pilgrims who came to pray for some sick person they loved, or in the hope of being cured themselves. If he were to find out now that he was the fool, and not they.... Well, suppose you owned a cow, Mark, and had milked her every day for years, and had shoveled out her stall when you felt like it; then suppose you discovered that that cow was really a being more pow- erful and noble than you could comprehend, who had been allowing you, because of her generosity, to have the milk. How would you feel?"

The abbé cleared his throat self-consciously. "We've been over the whole building now, I think; that ceiling you're rapping is only the floor of the storage room we were in a few moments ago. Don't you think we'd better go back to the tap and see how the others are?"

Mark agreed reluctantly and followed the abbé out. Once he said, "They could be in the stable or one of the sheds, I suppose."

The abbé looked back at him. "I thought you told me Josellen's father said they were in this building?"

"I think he did," Mark said. "Only, they just aren't."

"Let's use our heads as well as our feet, before we be- come certain about that," the abbé suggested as they went into the firelit taproom again. To Mother Cloot he called, "Find out anything, old woman?"

She was on her knees at the paralyzed man's feet when they came in, so that for a moment Mark wondered if she were not saying a rosary for him. Then he saw one of her clawlike hands sweep the hearth in a familiar gesture and realized with a shiver of fear that she had been casting the runes.

"No," she said as she turned around, now squatting on her heels, to face the abbé. "Not about the weaver and the girl I haven't. I've learned something else, though."

"With those?" The abbé snorted in disgust. "What did she do, Cope?"

From his seat at one of the tables Cope said, "Whispered to him for a while, Father. I went into the kitchen for a moment to see if Philip's wife was still there, and when I came out, she had the poker out of the fire and had touched it to his feet. I took it away from her and gave her a shaking, but it's really not much of a burn, and I don't believe he feels it anyway. I rubbed some lard on it, and he didn't seem to notice. Then she began tossing those things on the hearth."

"I know who broke his head and took the movement and feeling from his limbs," Mother Cloot said suddenly, "and I'll tell you now."

Mark looked at Cope and knew too.

"Cope did it! With one of his big hammers or some other tool he had—"

She was interrupted. Cope said, "Only a wooden board I had in my kitchen to chop meat on." He had buried his face in his big hands.

Mother Cloot was obviously surprised by his sudden

confession, but she tried to continue. "The innkeeper came to him, and they fought again. Cope would have killed him before, the night Wat was here, if no one had been watching."

"I only wanted to hit him, not to kill him," Cope said. "That time or the other. He came to my house this morning and began asking about you, Abbé—if I knew where you were or how he might get a message to you. And I thought to myself, 'So you've sold us to the soldiers now, like you sold us to Wat.' I wouldn't answer him, but he kept guessing and guessing until he was nearly at the truth."

"There!" By a considerable effort Mother Cloot raised herself to her full height, a dark figure in front of the blazing fireplace. "He says so himself. Now what do you plan to do?"

"Nothing." The abbé had taken a seat while Cope was speaking; he now stretched his legs out and leaned back in it to look more easily at Mother Cloot.

"About murder?"

"It isn't murder," Mark hedged. "He isn't dead."

"Oh, isn't he?" The old woman sucked new breath past her mucus. "You come and look."

Mark and the abbé did so. The innkeeper's eyes were still open and staring, but blindly, like the wooden image worshiped by the charcoal burners. On the side away from the fire his flesh felt cool to the touch already. The abbé closed the eyelids firmly with his fingers, pulling both down at the same time, and to Mark's relief they stayed down. The arms, which had been lying by the innkeeper's sides, he crossed ritually just above the dead man's paunch. There was nothing in the room to cover him with except the blanket in which he had been wrapped. Drawn over

his face, it left his feet, in gray woolen stockings, protrud-
ing from the bottom.

"Now," the abbé said, looking at Mother Cloot, "I tried
once to have him make you leave this room. He wouldn't
do it, but he is no longer here to prevent me from doing it
myself. You get out of here and go back to wherever it is
you belong, or I'll throw you out bodily. Understand?"

As the haggard old woman began edging toward the
door, he added, "And one other thing: no curses. Not
within my hearing. I happen to credit the efficacy of the
powers to whom they're addressed even though I question
the efficiency of what's said." After she had left, he barred
the door behind her, saying, "Cope, you might carry him
in to where Susan's lying when you feel well enough to do
it." Then he resumed his chair and sat quietly for some
time, unobtrusively watching Cope, whose face was still
plunged in his hands.

Mark had eaten the apples he had brought from the
kitchen before the search of the inn, but now he began to
wish heartily that he had something further. He realized
the impossibility of eating in the presence of Cope's grief,
but after a time it occurred to him that he might pass off
a visit to the kitchen as an inquiry after Philip's wife and
that such an inquiry might in fact be called for. Neither
man took any notice of him as he left.

In the kitchen the fat woman had fallen asleep on her
little stool. Her head was so propped by the flesh of her
neck that it was nearly upright, and the bulk of her body
leaned back into the corner. She was snoring softly. Of the
several candles that had been burning in the room earlier,
only one guttering stump remained. Mark searched until
he found more to light from this, and then in an unaccus-

tomed burst of virtue he kindled the kitchen fire. He had picked up food as he went along in his hunt for candles and tinder, so after warming himself for a few minutes, he mounted the little stair leading to the taproom. Fortunately he looked through the doorway before he went in. Cope was kneeling beside the abbé's chair, and a cross on a chain, presumably the abbé's, had been hung from the back of the chair so that it was nearly level with the smith's eyes. The abbé was twisted in his seat to a position facing half away. Mark knew an impromptu confession when he saw one and dodged hurriedly back into the kitchen to finish his meal.

After what seemed a reasonable time he went up again; both Cope and the innkeeper's body were gone. The abbé had thrown fresh wood on the fire, and was engaged in levering the new logs into the most favorable positions with the poker. He smiled at Mark as he entered.

"Get yourself something to eat? How's the woman?"

Mark held out the bread and meat he had brought up from the kitchen. "She's all right; she's asleep. You must be hungry yourself, Abbé."

"I am that. Cope fed me well while I was with him— I used the anvil for a table, Mark, so as not to disturb the tools on his bench—but the last of those meals has been quite a while in the past."

"I guess that when he killed Josellen's father it was in the house, and you being in the forge didn't hear it?"

The abbé nodded with his mouth full, then took a heroic swallow. "I didn't even know the man had come. Poor Cope thought it was to spy me out for the soldiers, but I imagine it was really to try to bring me to Gloin that he came."

"Do you really think Gloin is hurt so badly?"

"How should I know?" The abbé shrugged his shoulders and took another bite of his sandwich. "There's many a man walking and whistling," he continued through the mouthful, "who's had the last rites three or four times. Don't lose heart."

"We should have had Mother Cloot cast runes for us," Mark said despondently. "She could have found out where they are."

"You don't still believe in that, do you? You're forgetting that it was just *that* information she set herself to find when we went to search the inn."

"She found out about Cope."

"That's not difficult. I'm surprised you didn't see it yourself."

"You mean a person could just guess it?" Mark looked incredulous.

"Certainly. Just as Mother Cloot did. After all, who was available to strike the blow, eh? Myself, most unlikely to anyone who knows me at all. The soldiers, including the man you call the Boar, and perhaps this Sieur Ganelon. And you, Gloin, Josellen, and Cope. Somewhere out in the forest, Wat and his friend. Can you think of any other?"

Mark shook his head. "I can see why most are out, but why couldn't it have been the Boar and his men?"

"Ah!" The abbé nodded rapidly. "There you have a point. Make no mistake, it *could* have been them, which is why only an irresponsible person like Mother Cloot would have made the accusation with so little evidence. But would the soldiers have killed a man, leaving him dying at their own back door—which is what the stable gate was, nearly—then lied about it? No, they're practical fellows. They'd either have boasted of the killing to terrorize us, if they thought themselves safe from the law, or have finished him off and buried the body in the wood. And of course Mother Cloot would have considered how unlikely it was that he suffered his injury at the spot where he was found. Had you thought of that?"

"No, I hadn't, and I'm not sure I see it now."

"If the soldiers had done it, she would think, it would almost certainly have been inside the inn, since both they and he were living in the building. If someone else did it, he'd be unlikely to strike so close to where the soldiers were. Therefore it was quite probable he was carried to where he was found—a spot as close to his inn as his attacker dared to take him. He was a man of fair height and quite portly. Whom does that suggest as a carrier?"

"Cope for his strength, of course." Mark was secretly angry at himself for not having seen through the simple problem sooner.

"One last point. He was clubbed on the head, not stabbed or cut with a sword as he almost surely would have been by the soldiers or Sieur Ganelon or Wat. And he was not actually *killed*, but brought alive to a point close to his home, suggesting, certainly, a blow struck in anger by someone who later regretted his act."

"Had you worked all this out before?"

The abbé nodded. "While Cope was going to get you. I wouldn't have felt so certain if it hadn't been for Cope's dejected bearing. Surely you must have noticed it too."

"Well . . ." Mark hesitated. "What are we going to do now?" He tried to imagine the abbé and himself subduing the powerful blacksmith and failed utterly.

"About Cope? Nothing at all. Why should we?"

Mark groped hopelessly. "He killed Josellen's father."

"Who cannot be restored to life—at least not by us. Certainly not by hanging Cope. Do you think Cope would kill him again if he had this day to live over?"

"No." Mark thought of Cope as he had last seen him, kneeling by the abbé's chair. "No, he wouldn't."

"Do you think that in the future he will be a danger to the rest of us? Or will he be slower to strike than the common run of men?"

"You mean it won't benefit anyone to kill him. But what about justice?"

"Leave justice to God, Mark. We have no right to sit in His seat. Men have only the right to protect themselves from a brother man whom they have good reason to think dangerous. And the divine privilege of being merciful."

"What will we tell Josellen?" For a moment the prospect of breaking the news to Josellen seemed so repellent to Mark that he almost wished she too were dead.

"I don't believe we will have to tell her anything. That is one of Cope's penances. But we have to find her first, so I want you to think over everything her father told you. When you have it all straight, describe to me what must have happened to her from the time the soldiers arrested you at the camp until the time her father went to Cope's."

"All right. First of all, Josellen bit a soldier on the hand—I saw her—and got away. Gloin must have gotten away at the same time, and they met somewhere in the forest. Then Gloin was shot with an arrow."

"Stop a moment." The abbé raised one hand. "Was he shot soon after they left the camp?"

"Josellen's father didn't say; but now that I think of it, it must have been, because Gloin thought it was the soldiers who did it. Also, it took them a long time to get back here. They didn't get here until the soldiers took me out of the cellar to question."

"Were you told where the wound was?"

Mark shook his head.

"The long, slow journey suggests the leg or foot," the abbé said reflectively. "Obviously it wasn't bad enough to kill him quickly, and a man shot through the body usually either bleeds to death inside an hour or two or can move about pretty spryly before he turns feverish and pussy. It might have been that Josellen's father was trying to fetch me more as a leech than as a priest, you know."

"I hope so. Anyway, they came in late. They must have managed to attract his attention somehow. The Boar was busy with me, and I suppose most of the others were asleep. I know Josellen's father was up, though, because the Boar made him bring me food and both of us some wine."

"And then what?"

"Well, he hid them."

"Where?"

Mark could only look blank.

"Think back to last night—how you felt and how he must have felt. You knew him much better than I; he practically never came to the chapel except for a wedding or a funeral. Was he frightened of the men-at-arms?"

"He looked like it, and his lip had been cut by a fist. He told me they had beaten him pretty badly when they found out Josie was gone. I suppose he had seen Philip, too."

"In that case I should think he would have been half terrified," the abbé said thoughtfully. "I saw Philip when they marched him past the forge, and he looked bad enough then."

"If I had been him . . ." Mark tried to put himself in the place of the innkeeper—not the alternately roaring and unctuous authority of whom he had been in fear when he went to beg apples from Josellen, but the real man who had carried his tray into the inn parlor. And he thought of cocky, cheeky Josellen—now frightened, desperate Josellen—bringing the wounded Gloin into the inn late at night.

He looked across at the abbé still sitting with his forehead tensed by concentration, and felt for the first time the thrill of superior knowledge, the masterful buoyancy of having outmatched a really able mind. "Abbé," he said, "I know where they are."

The abbé looked up quickly. "You're sure?"

Mark nodded. "They're in the only room in the inn we didn't search." As much as he respected the abbé, he enjoyed enormously the puzzlement that flickered across his face.

"I'm certain you mean more than the trivial proposition of logic," the abbé said. "What is it?"

"Let's go let them out." Mark had picked up a candle already and was going toward the door. "I'll explain as we go."

"Go on." The abbé caught up with him.

"He was afraid of what would happen to him if the soldiers found out he'd hidden them, so he hid them in the place that would protect him perfectly if they were found. In the same cellar where Philip and I and Philip's wife and Old Sue had been locked up. You see, if they had been found there, he would have said to the Boar, 'I knew you

wanted them, sire, but you were busy and your men sleeping, so I just put them in with the others.' Of course he
showed them where to hide and probably gave them blankets and food and so on before he put them in. An ordi-
nary person wouldn't have followed his instructions, of
course."

"But Josellen was his daughter," the abbé added for him
as they strode down the hall, "and Gloin was probably so
weak he'd do anything he was told in order to get a place
to lie down. . . . But I went in there myself to look at
Susan's body, don't forget; besides, Philip and his wife
must both have been there when they came in."

"Philip had been beaten half to death," Mark said,
"and his wife would have been crying and holding him in
her arms in the dark. All Josellen's father had to do was
put out any lights they might have had before he opened
the door. Then he led them through the front part of the
cellar and hid them behind the pile of old wood toward the
back."

They had reached the stairway leading to the cellar in
which the prisoners had been confined, and in the light
of the candle Mark pointed toward the door at the bottom.
"See the drop latch? I noticed it when they first brought
me here, and I guess it's one of the reasons the Boar decided to use this cellar for prisoners. After Cope had taken
Sue's body out of here, Josellen and Gloin couldn't get out
even if they had realized the soldiers were gone. When you
came in, or when Cope did twice—once to let Philip's wife
out and once to bring Sue up—I don't suppose there was
much said, and the lights and the noise of the door would
have made them get down and be quiet. Anyway, even if
Josie had known it was you and Cope, she probably

wouldn't have let you know she and Gloin were in there. When we were caught at the camp, everybody thought you'd told where we were; she'd wait for her father to come back and say that things were safe." He pulled the door open as he ended his explanation and called, "Josie, it's all right now," into the darkness.

After a moment they heard the sound of feet, and the girl called softly, "Mark?"

19

THEY HAD SLEPT in the inn that night: Mark, Cope, the abbé, and the injured Gloin in the taproom; Josellen and Philip's wife in the kitchen. There had been no reason why they should not have used the guest rooms of the inn, and still less why Gloin and Mark or the abbé or Cope should not have gone to their own homes. But they did not. Instead Mark and Josellen had carried in bedding while the abbé dizzied Gloin with wine and treated his leg wound as best he could.

The arrow had entered his thigh just below the hip and struck the bone. When Josellen had attempted to extract it, the shaft—that of a hunting arrow from her description, not of a military crossbow quarrel—had separated from the iron head. That night the abbé had reopened and cleaned the wound, but when he had tried to draw out the head with tongs, it had broken and left its point still embedded in the bone.

Watching the process, Mark had realized for the first time on what easy terms he had survived Wat's knife thrust. Gloin's skin was the gray color of wool, and all the substance seemed to have been drained from him, leaving the cords of his neck and the veins of his face standing out like the branches of a winter-stripped bush; he had screamed when the abbé tugged at the arrowhead, though he had bitten his lips until they ran with blood in the attempt not to.

Afterward the abbé had gone to the wine cellar himself to bring Gloin another great ale-jack of strong wine, but Mark knew that the weaver had slept very little.

Now with light in the windows, the taproom suddenly seemed filled with stale odors. Mark threw off his blankets and stood close to the remains of the fire to warm himself while he studied those who still slept. Cope, he knew, had spent most of the night beside Josellen's father's corpse, and he looked it. There was dark flesh under his eyes, and his big, childlike face sagged. Asleep, the abbé seemed younger—perhaps because of the relaxation of intellectual effort. He was handsome in an ascetic fashion. Gloin's face could not be seen; the weaver lay on his side with his blankets drawn over his head, looking no larger than a boy. The blankets twitched as Mark watched, then were quiet again.

Walking carefully so as not to disturb the others, Mark made his way out of the tap to the steps of the inn, where the rising sun came straight down the village street to bathe him in new yellow warmth. It was cold in the shadows, he found, but the wind had died during the night. He turned his back to the sun and felt it comforting his shoulder blades, then broke a green twig from an elm to worry into a teeth cleaner. The faintly bitter taste was fresh in his sleep-furred mouth. He scrubbed away with the frizzled end of the twig and spat repeatedly with enjoyment. After completing the operation, he strolled to the stream behind the inn to wash his mouth with water.

When he returned to the steps, Josellen was there with a bulky brown bundle in her arms. She waved to him, and he waved back. She, too, had been crying in the night, he felt certain. It showed in the inflammation of her eyes and, unromantically, her nose; but it was not apparent in her demeanor now.

When he was close enough to talk without disturbing the people asleep inside, he said, "Good morning, Josie. Did you pass a good night?" For some reason he could not explain even to himself, he felt a need for formality, and it was apparent in his choice of words.

She nodded and said, "I brought you this; I thought you'd like it." She handed him the bundle she carried, pushing it at him suddenly.

He unfolded it. It was a sheepskin coat. Made with the fleeces turned in and the leather of the outside tanned and then greased with mutton fat to make it supple and water shedding, it was the kind of coat worn in winter by every shepherd. This was a good one, and though he could see that it had been worn at least one season before, it was still almost new. A broad extension of the back skin could be turned down to form a generous collar with the fleece side out.

"I cleaned the outside"—she ran her fingers over the leather—"with whipped-up egg whites last spring. It came out nice, didn't it? Put it on."

He did so. The sleeves were a bit long, the front monstrous—so voluminous he could almost wrap it about himself twice.

"I'll take it in. I just wanted to see how much to take."

"Don't bring it up too tight," he warned her seriously. "I'll grow yet, and don't forget I'll be wearing other stuff under it when it's really cold." He remembered the raw red wrists of winter. "Don't take the sleeves up *any*."

"I won't. I'll leave plenty." She looked at the coat critically. "How old are you now, Mark? I forget when your birthday comes."

"Fifteen." It was a lie, but only by six weeks or so. Besides, Gloin himself was uncertain about what year he had been told Mark had been born in.

"You look more than that. You're almost man-high right now."

"I don't feel that way." He seated himself on the top step and opened out the coat, offering Josellen a place on his left in the ample folds.

"That's because you've been around the abbé lately, and Cope." She seated herself next to him, pressing her side against his and allowing him to wrap her back in the sheepskin. "The abbé is terribly tall, and Cope's almost a giant. You're nearly as big as most men ever get right now."

"I suppose so, but I haven't got much beard yet, and Gloin says you don't stop getting taller until your beard comes in strong." She had slipped her arm around his waist inside the coat as a means of sitting closer, and his arm around her shoulders brought one face of her full right breast into contact with his side. He was acutely conscious of it.

"You're so fair your beard won't show much when it does come in." She was silent for a moment. A stray puff of wind tossed an autumn leaf—dead, clear yellow, and crackly—against his chest. He brushed it aside.

"Do you think anyone else is awake in there?" he asked.

She shook her head. "Philip's wife is going to sleep all day, I think. She slept like she was drunk all night—just lay there on her back, you know. I was going to say"—the girl hesitated—"that she slept like the dead. But the dead people, my father and Sue, seem sort of awake, really. Maybe it's because you can't hear them breathing."

"I know what you mean."

"Cope kept candles burning in there with them all night, you know. It was good of him, but we're about to run out of candles. My father always bought them when he went into town for the fair, so we're almost out now."

"So did the abbé," Mark said. "Holy candles for the church, I mean."

He wished he could touch her thigh. He was aware that if he did not call attention to it, she would permit it; but when he brought his arm around in front of him, the stiff, inflexible sleeve of the coat moved up to cover his fingers. Around his waist her arm tightened very slightly.

20

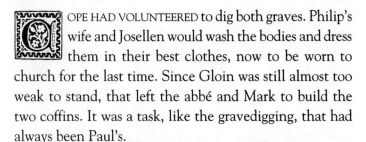OPE HAD VOLUNTEERED to dig both graves. Philip's wife and Josellen would wash the bodies and dress them in their best clothes, now to be worn to church for the last time. Since Gloin was still almost too weak to stand, that left the abbé and Mark to build the two coffins. It was a task, like the gravedigging, that had always been Paul's.

The tools and wood were in a shed behind the abbé's house. It was fortunate that there was a good supply of wood; sawing the planks from logs was the biggest job of all, as even Mark, who knew little of carpentry, realized. Even with the planks already made for them, it seemed unlikely to him that they could build anything with the few worn tools on Paul's bench. The abbé, however, seemed to feel no such doubts. He was selecting likely planks with an air of considerable confidence. Holding up a piece for Mark's inspection, he said, "This is birch, I think. Do you know anything about wood, Mark?"

Mark shook his head. "I know more about wool, Abbé.

I can tell oak from maple, but that's nearly the end of it."

"You ought to learn. You're young, so anything you learn now will be there to use for most of your life. Besides, wood and carpentry are interesting in themselves, and were the profession of Our Lord from the time He was old enough to help His foster father. Have you ever thought of Him as a little child playing with sawdust and shavings? No doubt He did."

Mark ran his hand over the abbé's white plank. "That's birch?"

"I think so. Paul sawed up a birch about two years ago, and although most of it seems to have been used, it appears there are still a few bits left. It's an easy wood to work, which is good, since you and I will probably need every help. Do you have the measurements?"

Mark showed him a piece of twine he had knotted to indicate the heights of the two people they were to bury. The abbé held his board up to it and found it to be a hand's breadth longer than the distance from the end to the first knot. "This will make a good backpiece for Susan then," he said ruminatively as he laid the board on the workbench. "Strange that I should be making *her* bed at last, isn't it? After all the beds she's made for me?"

The two coffins took them the better part of the day to build, though they were nothing but bare wooden boxes large enough to hold the bodies. Several times a plank split as Mark drove in the last nail—square and made by hand by Cope, who found nail manufacture a profitable way of keeping busy when there were no horses to be shod or any jobbing ironwork to do. He shamed himself on one of these occasions by swearing, but the abbé only said, "You should try this with pegs; you wouldn't curse nails then."

And the abbé showed him the auger he would have had to make every peg hole with.

When Cope finished the graves, he went home to put on clean clothing for the funeral mass, but when he returned to the chapel and found them still working, he gave them a hand with the last of the joining. Mark could not help thinking that things would have gone faster had he and the abbé dug the graves and Cope, with his aptitude for tools, built the coffins. Finally both boxes were complete, and they rubbed them down with the oil pressed from flax seed, which gave the wood a pleasant golden color and a sweet odor, and would repel water.

Later Mark found it strange to see his own handiwork beside the altar in the chapel. He had been to requiems often before, since Gloin insisted upon their both attending whenever any of the shepherds with whom he did business, or any of their families, died. He had never paid any particular attention to the coffins, never reflected that Paul had spent hours making them and that while Paul sat in the last row in his clean, worn clothes, he knew he would soon be burying his work, never to be seen again. At the altar the abbé moved through the mysterious gestures of the mass. His fingers made crosses in the air, and he spoke in a language Mark had been told was Latin. A slanting shaft of sunlight found one of the places where Mark had swung his hammer too hard and left a depression in the wood. He wondered if anyone else saw it.

When the ceremony was over, he and Cope carried the coffins out one at a time, he taking the feet and Cope the head of each. Old Sue's was easy, so light he could hardly believe she lay inside; but Josellen's father's strained his arms almost unbearably. Although they tried to lower it decently, it seemed to lunge into the grave, and struck the earth at the bottom with a thump. Beside it the wooden cross that marked Josellen's mother's grave leaned over to peer down into the hole. Seeing that reminded Mark with unexpected vividness of the woman he had almost forgotten: her height and rigid awkwardness, her worn look in afternoon sunlight. He tried to imagine what her body must be like by now. How far? Two feet from her husband's new grave?

Old Sue went in quietly, with the stiff decorum everyone expected of her when she had just been to church. Near hers, Paul's grave was still graceless and grassless, with an unweathered cross. When he looked up from lowering Sue's coffin, Mark saw Mother Cloot standing behind the mourners, apparently unnoticed by them and by the abbé as well.

It was understandable enough that she should come; Old Sue had been one of the last links with her own girlhood. Still, there was no look of sorrow on her raddled face, but rather an expression of cunning and expectancy. Was it possible that she intended to disinter her friend's body later, as it seemed the sexton's corpse had been exhumed from whatever grave his murderer had dug for him? Witches, Mark knew, were supposed to use corpse-fat for various purposes, but he had the idea that virgins and the unbaptized and the hanged were the favored sources. Besides, he thought practically as he straightened up, Old Sue would provide very little fat of any kind. Perhaps it was Josellen's father's grave Mother Cloot had come to see.

The abbé sprinkled the first earth on Sue's coffin lid. Mark noticed that his eyes were bright with tears, and the boy was still young enough to be embarrassed by the knowledge. Cope—Mark decided Cope had not seen Mother Cloot yet either—picked up his spade and began to fill the grave in earnest. Mark remembered how everyone at the peddler's funeral had relaxed when the top of the coffin had been covered, and he watched to see if the same thing would happen now. It did, but not so markedly. There was some real grief here as well as the common determination to do duty by the dead.

The abbé had perfect control of his face, but the tears came alternately from eye and eye to run down the sides of his nose until they were channeled into the deeply graved lines that led to the corners of his mouth. Cope, filling Sue's grave still, looked only tired. Philip's wife was crying. Josellen was bravely not crying, but seemed ready to begin when everything was over.

Cope took up one of the two wooden crosses they had prepared, then looked at the abbé, who nodded reassurance that the name cut there was Susan's. Cope leaned his weight on it and pushed it into the soft ground.

An arrow struck the wood just beneath his fingers.

Thirty years afterward, when faces and even names had grown vague, Mark could still close his eyes and see that arrow fletched with gray goose feathers trembling ever so slightly just under the blacksmith's hand. It told him, thirty years afterward when he had time to think about such things, that events do not vanish with passing time but remain new and unceasing in the comprehension of God forever. The arrow still quivered, fresh shot, in the new raw wood of the cross—somewhere.

Surprisingly it did not seem to occur to any of them to duck. They only turned to look in the direction from which the arrow had come, making easy targets, as Mark realized later, for any further shots. There were none; but dirty, ragged men with bows and spears and axes were stepping out of the trees circling the chapel yard. Wat stood in the center of them with his bow in his hand. He was grinning, or at least his lips were drawn back from his teeth, and he held another arrow ready to nock.

Somehow Mark expected him to make some jesting remark about being late for the funeral or happy to see them all again, but he did not. He merely waited until his men were deployed around him—Mark counted nine including Gil—then came walking toward them with long, slow strides.

The abbé said, "What do you want here?"

Wat was looking at Cope and seemed not to hear. When he had come to within fifteen feet, he halted. There was something unnatural in Wat's eyes that reminded Mark of the way Mother Cloot looked at times; he waited a long while before he said thickly to Cope, "Do you want to fight? I'll give you a knife if you want to fight."

Beside him Gil hefted his ax. Mark saw the smith's eyes travel from Wat to the charcoal burner and back, then to the ring of other burners farther off. "No. No, I don't want to fight. What do you want us to do?"

"Start walking back to the village. The abbé will walk behind you, and the others behind him. No looking back and no bolting for the wood."

Mark let Philip's wife and Josellen go ahead of him, feeling somehow that this was the manly thing to do. Two burners were skirting the path on either side of Cope and about a pace back. Something in the way they moved and looked at the prisoners between them told Mark that they were eager for the killing to begin but did not want to begin it themselves. He started as Wat laid his muscular hands on his shoulders from behind.

In his ear Wat said, "Mark, are you awake?"

Not understanding what was meant, Mark could only nod.

"That's strange," Wat whispered. "I am dreaming, and you are awake in my dream." Mother Cloot touched his arm, and he said no more.

21

HEY WERE HALFWAY to the village when Mark ran. Between one step and another the knowledge that he was to be a prisoner again, that Josellen and Gloin would be prisoners too, that he would be utterly at the whim of Wat, who had tried once already to kill him, combined to stifle all prudence and all fear as well. At one moment he was looking at Josellen's back and her tossing red hair; the next, at the wind-shaken red leaves of the trees while shouts rang in his ears. He turned his head to look back, and as he did, an arrow passed—*whi-i-ick!* He saw Wat still in the position of having loosed, before his arm went to the quiver on his back for another shaft. At the head of the line Cope was turning ponderously, his arms coming up from his sides. Everything, including Mark himself, was in a swirl of motion that was yet divisible into sharply defined detail.

He somersaulted over a root, and the ground moved toward his face as the Boar's door had. He threw his hands forward and felt the sting in his palms an instant before his nose and right cheek struck. The breath was knocked out of him for only a heartbeat, but in that heartbeat he could feel in imagination the iron head of a spear at his back. He pushed himself away from the earth with his arms; Cope struggled in the midst of a knot of men, Mark thought with Wat's throat in his hands, though the swarming burners prevented him from seeing either man well. As he watched, someone, Gil, raised a flashing ax and brought it down. It was as though a great tree were falling, but the ax came up bloody. Mark scrambled to his feet and dove into the forest without waiting to see more.

Trees flashed past him and occasionally tore at his clothes. He jumped fallen logs as best he could, tried to keep a trunk always between himself and any pursuers, once knocked himself nearly unconscious on a low limb.

At last his run became a breathless trot, though for a time his mind strained to lash his muscles back to speed. His aching lungs got air again, and his dizziness and the roar of blood in his ears stopped. He slackened his trot to a walk, then halted to listen for sounds of pursuit. And when he had become accustomed to the silence of the forest and the far, faint sighing of the wind, he heard them.

Somewhere behind him feet were running, kicking the crisp leaves that covered the ground, now and then breaking through brush with a crackling burst. Several men, he thought. He began to run again. At the noise he made, there was a yell behind him like the distant yelp of a hound. He took the hint, slowed down, and tried to move as silently as he could in a direction at an angle to his former flight. After a few minutes he became sure that his pursuers had changed direction as well, and he shifted his own again.

Once, just before the sun set, he saw them. He had struck the riverbank and was running upstream along it, and at a point where the river made a long curve that edged away from him, he was able to look back and see them jogging along the path where he himself had been five minutes before. There were two. Both charcoal burners; both, he thought, taller than Gil. One carried a spear and the other an ax, and even as fear gripped him, he wondered why they pursued him so intently after several hours of trailing. Had Wat threatened them with death if they did not bring him back?

As night came, he turned away from the river, determined to take all the advantage he could from the deeper shadow under the trees. Again and again he halted and listened intently until he could hear, or thought he could hear, the two burners moving. Once they betrayed themselves by cursing, as they had by yelling before, but apparently they learned from that and did not repeat the mistake. The night seemed already to have lasted years when the moon, well past the full now but still a potent threat, rose and moved through a racing mob of strangely shaped clouds. Then it began to rain.

The rain ended all games of moving and listening. Lightly at first, then like hard-thrown, stinging pebbles, the drops beat the last leaves remaining on the trees and the thick-strewn leaves on the ground to make a rushing roar like the sound of a cataract. Mark was soaked to the skin in a moment, and though exercise had kept him warm until then, he was now freezing. He blundered on in the darkness, knowing that unless the burners actually touched him there could be no detection.

Once the groping fingers he held stretched before him

encountered a pillar of stone instead of the familiar, bark-clad shape of a tree trunk, and he knew himself to be at Miles Cross and could actually stand for a moment in the shelter of the huge flat stone that was its top. Shaking with cold in his clinging tunic, he wondered if the Barrow Man was out of his bed in the tumulus tonight, stalking the rain-swept forest paths in his green armor. The thought was more dreadful than anything Wat and the burners might do to him; he launched himself into the rain again.

The downpour slowed to a drizzle a little after dawn, leaving the sky full of hurtling clouds and the trees stripped bare, every red and brown leaf whipped to the ground by the flailing rain. He did not know in which direction to walk; so all ways were the same to him, and he went by the easiest.

The sun had been up for about an hour when he saw through the bare limbs a thin column of smoke far off. He turned toward it and began wearily to trot.

As he had hoped and somehow expected, the smoke was rising from the soldiers' breakfast fire. A ragged tent—surely not large enough for them all—had been pitched in a small clearing. A pot was bubbling on the fire with a delicious smell, and as he came up, one of the soldiers was ladling out bowls for the others. Even Philip was drinking already from a cup taken first off the pot where the broth was thinnest. The Boar stood, bowl in hand, waiting for the last ladleful, which would hold most of the meat.

Mark had come nearly to the fire before any of them saw him. He dropped to one knee in front of the Boar, whose eyes narrowed at the sight of him. "I know . . ." Mark tapped himself on the chest, gasping for breath. "I know where Wat is. I'll guide you and help you."

One of the soldiers swore in surprise.

"But you have to promise me. Not to hurt Josellen or Gloin or any of the other people in our village. I think Cope's dead. Not to burn any more houses."

"You shouldn't kneel and then strike bargains," the Boar said. He was grinning, the protuberant tooth more noticeable than ever. "It ain't the way to do it. You're sure about Wat?"

"I left him late yesterday. I've been in the wood all night, and two of his men are trying to catch me. Will you take him no matter who he is?"

"Why, Wat is Wat, ain't he? Of course we will." The Boar lifted Mark up by the front of his tunic. "Now, what was those pledges you wanted? Don't make them too stiff, or we'll find if a coal from the fire might not take them down a bit."

Mark's knees felt weak, just as they had when Wat had stabbed him and he had lost so much blood; but he managed to stand up and say what he had to staunchly enough. "No harm to Philip's wife or Gloin or the abbé, or Cope if he's still alive. No rape or hurt to Josellen. No more setting fire to houses. Or the inn or the chapel," he added as an afterthought. "And a coal won't get you anything."

The Boar laughed at that, and most of the soldiers joined in. "Well, that's manly enough, and reasonable for catching Wat and getting out of this damp. Don't you even want your cobbler back?"

Mark had not given any thought to making Philip a part of the price for Wat's arrest, and it took him a moment to get accustomed to the idea. "Yes," he said. "Yes, if you'll give him to me. He didn't do anything."

The Boar shook his head. "But you wouldn't stand to the fire for him, would you? I know you won't, so I won't let him go. Besides, certain people already know I've got him, so I couldn't if I would. I'll swear the rest on my blade, though." He drew his heavy sword and held it up before him so the hilt formed a cross. "And I'll give you a bowl of stew in the bargain. But you must leave us our comic cobbler, who's forever telling us how we'll all be punished for what we've done to him, and how Sieur Ganelon will see that he gets a new house. My lads enjoy having him about. Now, what's this about Wat's men? How many has he?"

"He had two of them chasing me in the wood last night. He's got nine altogether, counting Gil." Someone pressed a wooden bowl of steaming broth into Mark's hands, and he drank gratefully.

The Boar was looking at him closely. "Do you know the names of any of their men besides this Gil? How are they armed?"

"I don't know any of the others, but they're charcoal burners. Some of them have spears and some, bows. Some, only axes. Wat has a bow and his sword."

"Have any of them harness or shields?"

"No shields. I don't know what *harness* means; they don't have horses."

"It's this." The Boar touched the ring-mail shirt he wore. "A defense."

"Oh, no. Only regular clothes."

"Well now." The Boar straightened up and looked about at his followers. "We're not afraid of any wood rabbits with axes, are we, men? They'll scatter as soon as they know we're upon them. And some nice bits of gold we'll get for bringing in Wat, and we'll get out of this forest and back to the capital to boot."

Several of the soldiers nodded and growled agreement. Some of them were beginning to pack away belongings already.

"He's back at our village," Mark said.

No smoke rose from Cope's forge. Mark had hoped there would be some to tell him Cope was still alive, but he had known it was not true. Seen from the trees on the far side of the pilgrims' road, the forge already looked deserted. Behind it Cope's little house was still and empty, the door standing partly open as the blacksmith had left it to go to the requiem. Very faintly from the direction of the inn came the sound of voices.

"I do believe they're singing," the Boar said. He nudged a bearded soldier who had come up from the end of the column to stand next to him when they halted, and who was apparently his second-in-command.

The other nodded, and the Boar turned to Mark. "Can you take this man and two others back around behind that inn without them seeing you? I want to cut them off."

Mark nodded. "There're a lot of ways to get away from the inn, though. We couldn't watch them all."

"You could watch the main ones, couldn't you?"

Mark thought for a moment. "Gil told me once that when the burners come down the river they usually take their boats ashore at Grindwalled. We could block the way to that."

"That'll have to do." Looking back at his lieutenant, the Boar directed, "Take two who're good with their bows. I'll give you plenty of time to get into position, then rush

them right down the road. Remember, it don't matter a
bent farthing how many you get if you don't get Wat, or
how many get past if you do. Him first; then pick up whatever you can."

Mark led the three soldiers as well and as swiftly as he
could, making a wide circle of the village on the side away
from the stream and ending at a point from which they
could see the rooftree of the inn through the woods. Here
they halted while the bearded soldier looked over the
ground.

"This is bad," he said at length. "Too many trees for
those dirty burners to dodge behind and not enough visi-
bility. Is it any better closer up?"

"Not until you get almost to the inn. This path comes
around the side of it, and if you get close, you can see the
stableyard gate too."

"From how far off?"

One of the other soldiers said, "Fifty paces, maybe. I
was on picket back there for a while."

The bearded soldier seemed to approve of this, so they
moved cautiously up the path until they were in sight of
the stableyard. The sounds they had heard when they were
in the wood opposite Cope's forge were louder than ever,
and several times someone shrieked. As nearly as Mark
could judge, the noises came from in front of the inn. "I
wish the others would hurry up," he said.

"He wants to give us time to get set," the bearded soldier told him philosophically.

"We are set."

"He can't be sure of that. He has to give us plenty of
time."

"What do you think they're doing up there?"

"Getting coin from somebody. You heard him yell."

"There's no one who has money left," Mark said. In his own mind he counted off the men in the burners' hands; if Cope were dead, there were only two: the abbé and Gloin. He felt reasonably certain the screamer had not been Josellen or Philip's wife; the sound had not quite held the woman-note of shrillness.

One of the soldiers said, "What the Devil are they singing for?" and then the singing became a confused babble of voices. For a moment high, cracked shouts Mark felt certain must have come from Mother Cloot dominated the tumult; then even that semblance of order was swept away. The soldiers shifted slightly, moving farther apart and checking their weapons.

No one came. After holding himself tense for what seemed a long time, Mark relaxed, released his breath, and even took a step forward. A tall, thin man in ragged clothes ran around the corner of the inn and straight down the path toward them. His hands were empty, pumping alongside his waist as though he were running a footrace. His eyes and mouth were open to a grotesque diameter, and his shock of black hair was blown back from his face. The soldier to Mark's left brought up his crossbow, aimed, and released all in one smooth motion.

The quarrel struck just below the place where the ragged man's neck joined his shoulders. He bent forward as he ran, but kept running until it seemed miraculous he did not fall. Then, abruptly, as though he had succumbed to a sudden impulse to surrender, he sank to his knees and remained balanced there, staring at the dust of the path while the blood bubbled from his nostrils and mouth.

In front of the inn the yelling had ceased. The Boar's

voice came to them distinctly, readily identifiable through
the sound of others, though Mark could not understand
what it was he had said. The man in the path pitched forward on his face.

"I think that's all that's coming," the soldier with the
beard said. "That ain't Wat, is it?"

Mark shook his head.

"Come on then."

They walked around the dead man, past the ram-
shackle wooden wall that closed off the stableyard, and
turned the corner of the inn.

Mark's first impression was of a confusion of people in
which there seemed to be no groups, but only individuals
moving, crouching, or lying on the ground without regard
for any of the others. A soldier with a partisan was going
up the steps of the inn. The black-robed figure of Mother
Cloot crouched with head pressed to knees beside the
painted wooden image that was the charcoal burners' Virgin. A man whose blood oozed through rents in his tattered
shirt lay nearby. A strange woman, her face and shoulders
smeared with swirling streaks of ash, was weeping; her hair
was bound with plaited skeins of colored wool, and it was
not until Mark saw her eyes that he realized she was
Josellen.

From somewhere the Boar's voice demanded, "Did you
get anybody back there?" and the bearded soldier said
something in reply that Mark did not bother to listen to.
He put his arms around Josellen, and she pressed her face
against his chest.

Someone else was crying, and he was surprised to see
that it was Gloin. A soldier was dragging the weaver along
by one arm, and Gloin, who could hardly walk on his

wounded leg, was perhaps begging him to go slower; it was hard to tell.

Wat was walking toward them. It was a moment before Mark realized that this was because the Boar was behind him, prodding him with the point of a knife. One of Wat's arms hung so limply that Mark knew it must be broken, and blood ran down the sleeve and dripped from the ends of his fingers, yet no pain showed in the highwayman's expression; it was calm and aloof, detached from the shambles surrounding him. He looked toward the bowed figure of Mother Cloot as if for instructions or advice, but she did not lift her head. Mark tried to go over to ask the Boar to let him help Gloin, though he did not want to leave Josellen. He began to stroke her hair, trying to make her stop crying. Several of the soldiers were gaping at Wat.

22

OME IN, COME in," said the man in the armchair. "Don't stand there in the door half a league away where I have to shout at you."

Mark took a dozen steps forward and dropped to his knees. Behind him a resplendent warder closed the door, making a barely perceptible sighing noise as a quarter ton of carved oak swung through the still air.

The man in the armchair had a bottle and a goblet on a table in front of him. He filled the goblet with red wine before he spoke to Mark again. "Now then. You're the apprentice of this man Gloin, who was one of the bandit's spies and helpers, but you are not accused yourself. Is that correct?"

"Yes, sire." Mark shook his head. "I mean, no, sire. Gloin wasn't what you said, sire. But I was his apprentice."

"Then at least we've got that straight. You were brought to testify against him?"

"Against Wat, sire. Not against my master Gloin."

There was a fire at one side of the room, a huge blaze

in a fireplace that took up half the wall. Mark could feel the warmth where he knelt; it felt good after his long walk through the darkening city.

The man in the armchair smiled. "Let us say that you were brought to tell the truth. We can both agree on that, I take it? What did you say your name was?"

"Mark, sire."

"Very good." The man picked up a curling sheet of parchment, and seeing that he could read, Mark wondered if he were not a priest. His dark fur robe did nothing to dispel the idea, but his untonsured hair fell freely to his shoulders. "According to this report, the men dispatched to apprehend Wat the Wayfarer—I understand he was locally quite famous, is that correct?"

Mark nodded silently. It was incredible that Wat's reputation should not have reached this place.

"The soldiers sent to apprehend him and his confederates relate that they fought a pitched battle against Wat and his men in which they killed four and captured Wat himself, plus one Gloin, a weaver; one Gil, a charcoal burner; and one Philip, a cobbler—if the scribbler we had talk to them and write it up got things correctly." The man glanced up. "When one sends a clerk who can't think to get the report of a soldier who can't read, one takes one's chances.

"In addition, the following persons were brought as witnesses—well, to drop the formality, the priest of your village, yourself, a woman I understand to be this man Philip's wife, and a girl whose father was murdered by Wat. Where are you lodged, by the way?"

"In the Old Castle, sire, and it wasn't Wat that killed Josellen's father; it was Cope."

"You're in the prison? You're not supposed to be under arrest, only the first four names I read off. Surely they haven't put the priest in prison. His grace the archbishop would be screaming like the eagle of St. John."

"We're not chained up, sire. We have rooms with the warders, and the abbé is living at the friary."

"That's better. Come to think on it, I had a brief talk with your abbé yesterday, and he surely would have complained then if he didn't like his quarters. A very impressive man, with his gaunt face and that black bandage over his eyes; but he won't be of much use as a witness, I'm afraid. One can hardly have a man executed on a blind man's identification, though he could testify to the events before he lost his sight, of course. What do you know about the woman who blinded him?"

"He told me while they were taking us to the city that it was Mother Cloot, sire. He'd hidden the communion service when the soldiers came, and she told Wat she could find out where it was. Part of it was gold, sire. She put a spell on Wat."

"At least that's what Wat says, eh? Very convenient for Wat, since the woman isn't here to deny it. You seem to have known them both pretty well, Mark; what do you think? Did she do it—or could she?"

Mark nodded. "I think so, sire. Wat seemed unlike himself when he came out of the woods with the burners, and he told me he was dreaming. He said that it was real for me but a dream for him. I think the Barrow Man had put a spell on everyone except maybe Mother Cloot."

The man in the armchair looked angry. "I've no time for children's tales, Mark. Witchcraft may be one thing, but fairy stories are another. This Mother Cloot is supposed to have carried some sort of magic herb in a bag hung around her neck. What do you know of that?"

"She had something there, sire. I know that when she was tired she would take something out and chew it and be fresh again, but it made her eyes look strange, as if she had gone blind, sire. But about the Barrow Man . . ."

"Yes? Come out with it if you must."

"When the soldiers put the charcoal burners' Virgin in the fire and the paint turned black, you could see it wasn't a woman at all under the paint, sire. It was a man's face. And they were getting Josellen ready to be his wife, sire. Gil told me that Mother Cloot had said it was because the Barrow Man hadn't had a wife in so long that things were so bad, and if they gave him one there'd be no more soldiers or taxgatherers anymore, and they could kill the deer again. She knew the wife was supposed to be Josellen because Josellen had climbed up on Miles Cross."

The man in the armchair shrugged and leaned back in his seat to take a sip of wine. "I'd forgotten just how superstitious you people are," he said. "I suppose if I were to poke about my own estates I'd find things not much better there. At any rate, one sees why the old woman wanted to blind your priest."

"He could have been cured if the soldiers would have let him wash his eyes in St. Agnes' well and then pray a vigil all night the way he wanted, sire. But they wouldn't wait, and made us all leave right away."

"Oh, no doubt he could. But knowing the state of the king's roads in winter, I sympathize with the soldiers' desire to be moving. It's snowing outside now, I understand?"

"It was when they brought me in, sire."

The window at the end of the room was paned with

pieces of greenish glass, each with a bull's-eye in the center where the blower had lifted his rod. Mark's interro-
gator swung open the iron frame for a moment to look
outside; Mark could see the snowflakes sifting down
against the dark sky.

"Good boar hunting weather tomorrow." The man
closed the window and walked over to the fire to warm his
hands. "I like to watch the snow falling on the city, but
it's cold. Did you see the way it was sticking to the cathe-
dral? No, you couldn't have from where you are. Beautiful. It's because of the carvings, of course; it rests on the
heads of all our stone angels and devils. How do you like
the city, Mark?"

"It's nice, sire, but not having any money makes it
hard when we see the men selling roasted apples and the
like."

"I daresay it does at that." A small gold coin struck the
floor just in front of Mark.

"I didn't mean that, sire. I was just talking."

"Of course you did. Half your mind was saying, 'I'm
only answering his question,' while the other half said,
'Perhaps he'll give me something.' Go ahead and put it in
your pocket; we're all like that. By the way, though, who
are 'we'?"

"Sire?"

" 'We see the men selling roasted apples.' Who are
'we'?"

"Oh. Josellen and I, sire."

"Aren't you frightened at the thought of buying apples
for the Barrow Man's bride?"

"I hadn't thought of it that way, sire."

"Well, don't. You'll only make yourself uncomfortable. You express yourself much better than most peasants, Mark, and seem to be an intelligent boy; have you ever chewed any of that herb of Mother Cloot's? The one Wat says she enchanted him with?"

Mark shook his head.

"I have. Ah, that surprised you, didn't it? These witch-women are brought into court from time to time, and we soon learn their recipes. I could teach you how to compound philters or brew poisons as well as your Mother Cloot could, although I make no claim to magic powers. I've chewed the herb as an experiment, and it produces a lightheaded feeling—as if one had drunk a cup of strong wine after fasting. Nothing more. I suppose it might be a good restorative for fatigue."

"You didn't have anyone there to say the words, sire."

"That's right." The man took his seat in the great armchair again. "I didn't have anyone there saying the words. And if I had, and all my mind disbelieved them, it wouldn't have mattered. But"—he shook a finger at Mark—"if only half my mind had disbelieved, I'd have been enthralled, perhaps, by the other half. Just as poor Wat was. So don't let half your mind think this girl belongs to the Barrow Man. It's a dangerous practice."

"I won't, sire."

"Poor Wat is an educated man. Did you know that?"

"He was at the seminary. He told me about it when we were going down the river with Gil."

"Mark, you make my head ache; who is Gil? Wait, I remember—one of Wat's accomplices; the second one, the charcoal burner."

"He killed Cope. He killed Paul the Sexton too. I was

thinking, one time while we were walking to the city, of how he killed Cope—seeing his ax come up and down and bite into Cope's head—and I remembered seeing Paul's wound, just the same. Gil went to the meeting in the taproom that same night, sire, and he had his ax with him, but of course no one thought anything of it. So the next time the soldiers let me get close to him I asked, and he told me he'd done it. He'd been asking questions of Paul for Wat, and Paul cursed him and turned his back. He could make a word hurt, Paul could, sire, and he told Gil the village men'd hang Wat."

"Very clever of you, from only having seen the body before burial, though I daresay the other murder is the one we'll try him for, since there seem to be eyewitnesses to that."

"I saw it after it was buried, sire. Paul's body; I mean after Gil buried it. You see, he told Wat what he'd done when Wat met him at Mother Cloot's, and she overheard him and dug Paul up later—at least, that's what the abbé thinks—so she could make Old Sue think she had powers. It had rained, so I suppose the grave had sunk and was easy to find. She had hung him upside down in the shape of a cross to make it more mysterious."

The man in the armchair shook his head. "I'm not going to ask you who Old Sue is, Mark, and I don't want you to tell me; you're like the military engineer I met last week—you know so much about your subject that you can't explain it to anyone else. Let me ask you some direct questions instead, beginning with this one: Did you ever see Wat commit a murder or a robbery, you yourself being an eyewitness?"

"No, sire." Was Philip's money still where Wat had hidden it? he wondered. If he told now, Philip's wife would surely never see a glint of it.

"Did Wat ever confess to you that he had committed any murder or robbery?"

"He told me he killed the peddler, sire. The one that Cope found and the abbé and all of us buried."

"You saw the body yourself, and afterward Wat told you of his own will that he had done the murder?"

"Yes, sire."

"Fine. You've already told me about seeing this Gil murder a man, but now what can you tell me about the man called Philip the Cobbler? And your old master, this Gloin? What do you know of their misdeeds?"

"Nothing, sire, because they didn't do anything. Besides, the soldiers promised me that if I'd lead them to Wat they wouldn't harm Gloin, but when I did, they arrested him anyway."

The man in the armchair waved this away with a weary hand. "Let's talk about Wat for a moment. You told me you knew Wat had attended the seminary and was a well-educated man. He's still in minor orders, by the way, so there will be some dispute as to whether the civil or ecclesiastic courts hold jurisdiction. Anyway, what else do you know about him?"

"Only that he was born in the forest, sire. One of the poor people, and they all gave money to keep him in the seminary; I suppose they thought he'd be priest at the fountain someday."

"Yes. And it might seem that some of them, with their Barrow Man, may have had reasons other than local pride for wishing that. But Wat learned skepticism from reading devotionals, as so many of us do. A lot of the nobility send their sons to the seminaries just so that they will be strictly taught—did you know that, Mark? I suppose many of those young noblemen had a broad gold piece for every copper in Wat's pocket, and there's more to be bought in this city than roasted apples. If he *had* gone with the idea of serving the Barrow Man—whatever lost godling or folk hero *he* may be—Wat had learned to be skeptical of him too. But he had also learned that there are offices, and not such mean offices either, to which even a baseborn man may aspire if he has manners and money and old classroom friends of good blood. Do you understand me, Mark?"

"Yes, sire. I think so."

"Good. Now, just to satisfy my own curiosity, what are you going to do after this trial is over and you are free to do as you choose? How old are you?"

"Fifteen, sire. I'll go home and be Gloin's apprentice again, I suppose. My term's not out for two more years."

"And if Gloin isn't freed? You may take my word for it, by the way, that he won't be. The civil court will try him, and he'll be hanging in chains at some crossroads by the time this snow melts."

Mark's heart sank. After several moments of silence he said slowly, "I'll marry Josellen then, sire. We'll have the inn—though not many come—and Gloin's looms and combs, and I know the weaver's trade."

"That sounds fine. You've a place for life, Mark; I hope you appreciate that. You may go now. With the soldier to take you back to the Old Castle, you'll have an escort through our night streets, and I hope you appreciate that too; it's something many who are far richer than yourself might envy you."

Mark did not rise. "May I ask one question, sire? In favor?"

The man in the armchair said sharply, "What is it?"

"You said Wat didn't believe in the Barrow Man anymore, sire, but before that you said Mother Cloot's herb would work only if a person believed."

"Oh, is that all—I said Wat had become a skeptic, Mark. Half of him doubted; but half of him still wanted to believe and did believe, and that was enough. By believing, he wouldn't have to be afraid of the king's justice anymore, or of the king's soldiers either. And he desired that."

"But—"

"But most of all he wanted it to be true. Just as I, for example, want to believe in Christ and sometimes cannot."

"The Barrow Man is true, sire. I saw him in a dream come walking down our village street before I ever knew he was the Barrow Man, and then he really did, and the soldiers burned him there. I think Jesus is true too."

"You may go now, Mark."

The warder outside helped him open the heavy door, once he had pushed it enough to let the man know he was there. The Boar was sitting on a bench outside, apparently waiting to go in next. Light from the blazing cressets on the wall flickered redly on his polished steel cap.

Mark tried to walk past him without stopping, following the warder, but the Boar reached out and seized him by the arm. "Did you tell him?" he hissed. "Did you say anything?"

"About Wat being Sieur Ganelon?" Mark shook his head. "He knows, but he didn't want me to say it."

"Good. Your Wat had friends among the aristocracy. That would be when he was play-acting as Sieur Ganelon with the money he stole. It wouldn't do to embarrass them."

"I knew because of his bow," Mark said. "I mean, after I saw him at the inn. He had disguised his face, and even though I thought they were the same when I saw him, I wouldn't have believed it afterward. But he had left his bow at the inn when the soldiers came—and then he had it again, without ever having gone back to the inn. He had gotten it when he was Sieur Ganelon; he and Wat had to be the same person, no matter how strange it seemed."

"Well, watch your tongue, lad, if you want to get home safe. And be careful of your footing on the drawbridge—it was icing over when I crossed."

Mark ran to catch up with his warder, who was already a long way down the corridor.

Epilogue

ANY . . . *MIRACLES*," the man translated slowly, "*were performed here in medieval times. At least, I* suppose that word's *medieval*; can you make it out, dear?"

"You know I can't read the language. Less than you can, even, and least of all when it's cut in rock and all the Us have sharp bottoms like Vs and everything's all funny."

"*It is also . . . shrine*—should be *the shrine*, I suppose— *of Saint*—can't make out the name—*who recovered his sight here after being blinded by witches . . . and lived as a holy hermit and performed many wonderful cures.* That's all it says. Funny to think that our own ancestors came out of all this, isn't it? And not so long ago as history runs, either."

"My people came from Massachusetts," the woman said vaguely. "You get a lovely view of the Mountain from here, though."